EVERYTHING TO ME

BOOK 1 PLAYING FOR KEEPS SERIES

LAUREN FRASER

CONTENTS

BLURB

She's off-limits, but this pro-baller has never been one to follow rules.

Kendall Graves has been in love with her brother's friend for as long as she can remember. Unfortunately, he's never felt the same about her. She's always just been his buddy's annoying little sister. Until now.

When professional baseball player, Pete Saunders, agrees to let Kendall stay with him while she's in town, it never occurred to him she'd tempt him to break bro-code. Rule number 1- don't touch your friend/team-mate's sister. Rule number 2- see rule number 1.

But this Kendall is a whole lot different from the awkward little sister he remembered. This Kendall is sexy, stacked, and so freaking smart. It's enough to tempt anyone. And what his buddy doesn't know won't hurt him.

Casual he can do. Relationships? Not a chance. True love is just some crap people tell themselves so they don't have to be alone. He's not about to blow-up his whole life over something temporary. So why can't he stop thinking about her?

FREEBIE

Sign up for Lauren's newsletter and receive a free copy of Undercover Attraction. Join my mailing list for news of my latest release and sneak peaks at upcoming books and special newsletter only content.

Sign up at http://www.laurenfraser.com/newsletter

CHAPTER ONE

H oly cow, this was really happening. Today was the day she was finally going to get Pete Saunders out of her system once and for all. The man had been living in her head rent free for too long.

Kendall's hands trembled as she knocked on Pete's front door. Shifting her carry-on bag up her shoulder while she waited for him to answer, she mentally prepared herself for seeing him again. Taking a deep breath, she exhaled, trying to calm her nerves. *Oh boy.*

She couldn't believe she was staying at Pete's house, or that he'd agreed. When her brother, Ryan, had suggested she stay with his best friend while she was in town, she'd thought he was crazy. But the more she'd thought about it, the more it seemed like the perfect way to finally get over this stupid adolescent crush. *Well, here's hoping the reality lives up to her vivid imagination.*

The front door opened and her teenage crush stood before her, in the flesh, and even better than she remembered. The air whooshed out of her lungs at the first sight of him in his low-slung, gray sweatpants and threadbare Metallica t-shirt. She thought she'd been prepared. Clearly, she wasn't. What was it about this man that he always affected her like this?

Pete stared back at her, not saying anything, and she shifted nervously on her feet. "Hey. Sorry, I'm late. There were some issues with the plane."

"No problem," he replied. His green eyes scanned down her body, lingering on her waist, then back up. She licked her lips. Pete had never looked at her like this before. Like she was a woman and not just his friend's annoying little sister. Damn, it was a heady feeling.

She stepped forward and wrapped her arms around him. "Hi, thanks for letting me stay."

"Of course." He stepped back and looked down at her. "It's good to see you, Peanut."

And they were back. Whatever that brief look had been, it was gone. Now she was just Ryan's kid sister, Peanut.

"Can we not call me that? Please."

Pete's eyes twinkled as he smirked at her. "What? You don't like the nickname?" He chucked her on the chin. "It's cute 'cuz you're so little."

"I'm not that small," she grumbled.

Pete raised his eyebrow. "You're not very big."

She placed her hands on her hips and glared at him. "Next to you? No. But I'm 5′4. That's average, I'll have you know."

He chuckled and raised his hands up in defeat. "Sorry, my mistake."

She stepped past him and walked into the entrance-way. Her eyes were drawn to the exposed brick and wood beams. His place was beautiful, so warm and inviting. When she'd first pulled up to the older building, she'd expected some modern converted warehouse with lots of metal and white. But this was anything but that. "Wow," she murmured.

Pete smiled. "Come on in."

A calico cat popped out from behind the entranceway bench and wove its way around her legs. "Well, hello there. And who are you?" Kendall said as she bent down to scratch the fur behind the cat's ears.

"That's Mooch," Pete replied.

"Mooch? Seriously?"

"Yeah, it fits him perfectly. He looks all cute and innocent, but he's not. He's crafty." Pete narrowed his eyes as he looked at the cat in question.

"When did you get a cat? I thought you hated them." The boy she remembered had sided with Ryan to convince her parents not to allow her to get a cat when she was 15 because they smelled and were gross. Never in a million years would she have pictured him with one of his own.

"I do, but—" He bent down and scooped up Mooch. "He's not really mine."

"Oh no?" She eyed the cat tree in the corner of the room. "He looks like he's your cat."

"He's not. He's just recovering from an injury and needed a place to crash." He stroked his hand along the back flank of the cat and she saw the injury to his hind leg.

Kendall bit her cheek to hold in her laugh at his serious tone. "Gotcha, he's just a temporary roommate, then?" She walked closer to examine the stitches. "How'd he get hurt?" she asked.

"The vet wasn't sure, but thought maybe he'd been in a fight."

"The vet?" She smirked, then coughed to hide her amusement. "So, you took the cat that isn't yours to the vet?"

"Well..." Pete's ears turned red as he looked down at the ground. "He was hurt." He rubbed the back of his neck, his bicep flexing with the movement. "I couldn't just leave him."

She stroked the cat's ear and glanced up at Pete. Her heartbeat quickened the way it always did when she was close to her brother's good friend. He even smelled good. "How did you know he was hurt?"

He shrugged. "He came over to show me?"

Kendall snorted. "What do you mean, he came over to show you?"

Pete glanced at her and scowled. "He's been hanging around lately and he showed up yesterday morning and he looked pretty rough, so I took him to the vet. They had to put a drain in his leg so it doesn't get infected, and I couldn't just put him back on the street when it will need to be taken out in a few days."

"Of course not. So, you got a cat."

"No, it's just temporary." Pete scowled.

"And the cat tree?" she asked, indicating the elaborate tree in the corner.

"I didn't want him to get bored," Pete muttered.

Oh my god, could the man be any sweeter? She patted him on the shoulder. "I hate to break it to you, but I think you've got yourself a cat."

He glanced down at the cat in his arms. "Shit."

Kendall laughed. "All right, show me around this ridiculous place of yours." She looked at the high warehouse ceilings in the living room and over to the wooden staircase that led to what looked like additional rooms upstairs. "How did you find this place?" She trailed her hand along the smooth kitchen countertop. The kitchen was a cook's dream. She traced the lines in the quartz that made it look like marble. It was exactly the counters she would have chosen if she had her own home.

"You don't like it?" Pete asked.

"What? No, I love it, it's amazing."

"Oh, you said ridiculous, so I wasn't sure."

She squeezed his arm at the hint of vulnerability she heard in his voice. "I meant ridiculous in a good way."

Pete grinned, exposing his perfect white teeth. Her heart fluttered in her chest. It was no wonder he had all kinds of product endorsements. The man was gorgeous.

"Your brother thought I was an idiot when I bought this place."

"Yeah, well, my brother has no vision." She looked around the open floor plan of the warehouse. "Does this go right out to water?" She dashed towards the large sliding glass doors along the back wall.

"Yeah. I've got a dock with my boat right outside. It's perfect."

She looked at the wall of glass along the entire side of the space. "What about privacy?" she asked, pointing at the windows.

"One way glass. I can see out, but no one can see in."

"Oh, that's genius," she replied.

Pete waggled his eyebrows. "I'm not just a pretty face."

"Well, smart enough to buy a cool place when you see one," she teased.

"No, this was just a huge abandoned old warehouse when I bought it. That's why your brother thought I was nuts to want to live here. I had it converted into three separate units. I sold the other two, which paid for mine."

"Seriously?" She looked around the space with fresh eyes. Seeing everything about the place differently now that she knew Pete had a hand in creating the entire place. "I didn't know you knew how to do this kind of stuff."

He laughed. "I don't, but I'm smart enough to hire people who can build it the way I want."

"But you picked out everything and designed it?"

His face turned red and he shrugged. "I know what I like, so it's not that hard to hire people to do it when you have money."

"Do you have pictures of it from before?"

"Yeah." He grabbed her hand. Excitement zipped through her veins at the simple contact. Good lord, she really was like a schoolgirl around him. "Come here," he said as he tugged her towards a door on the left that led into a huge home gym. He stopped in front of a row of large, framed photographs of an old, rundown and grungy warehouse.

She leaned in closer to look at the pictures. "Is this it?" She trailed her fingers along the photo. It looked nothing like the place now. "Wow, Pete. This is amazing. I don't know how you looked at that and made this."

He laughed. "Again, I didn't make it. I hired people to make it." He looked around the room. "Well, this is

clearly the gym. Feel free to use it while you are here."
He glanced back at her. "You never said how long you
were here for."

"I think I'll be here a week. I hope that's okay."

"Yeah, of course it's fine. You can stay as long as you
need to," he told her.

They walked back out into the main living area, and
Pete gestured to the stairs along the right side of the
room. "Bedrooms are upstairs." He gestured for her to
go first.

"Are you helping Ryan with his renos, because he'd be
an idiot not to have asked your opinion after seeing this
place?"

"Yeah, I helped him with a few things. We have pretty
different taste."

Kendall snorted. That was putting it mildly. Her big
brother was a traditionalist. Ever since he was a little
boy and talked about making it to the major leagues,
he'd dreamed of having a big house with a gate that he
needed to buzz people into and the house had to have
a pool. When he'd finally bought his first home, those
things had still been on the top of the list. "I have to
admit, I thought I was a bit more traditional too, but now
that I've seen this place, I think you've converted me."

A smile split across Pete's face. "Yeah?"

"Oh my god, yes. Now show me the bedroom."

Silence filled the room. She glanced over at him and
the air crackled between them. He stared at her, then
cleared his throat and the moment was gone. "Right, I'll
show you to your room."

What had that been about? She'd had a crush on Pete
since the first time she'd laid eyes on him when she was

twelve years old and it had never gone away. If anything, over the years, her crush had grown. Now, being here in his space. Seeing what he created and getting this inside glimpse of the man he'd become. The crush would never go away. She'd always just assumed she didn't stand a chance, but if that look was anything to go by, maybe she did.

Conscious of Pete walking up the stairs behind her, she slowed down slightly and added a little extra sway to her hips. She heard him groan behind her.

"What was that?" she asked.

"Nothing. I just noticed the cat's toy is leaning against the built-in vacuum vent and I don't want to forget to move it before I turn it on."

"Gotcha." She smirked and flipped her brown hair over her shoulder. Seducing Pete Saunders just became her new mission while she was here. If he was interested in her in the least, there was no way she wasn't making the most of this trip.

At the top of the stairs, Pete brushed past her and walked into a large bedroom. A king-sized bed sat in the center of the room. Large windows looked out over the harbor. "One way glass in here too?" she asked.

"Of course." He picked up a remote from the bedside table. "You can add some extra tint to the windows as well if you don't like the sun beaming in. It's kind of like built-in blinds, but it's just a window filter." He set the remote down on the table. "I like being woken up to the morning sun, but I know not everyone does." He continued to walk deeper into the bedroom. "You have your own bathroom through here," he said, and led her through the doorway.

"Wow. This bathroom alone is as big as my bedroom at home." She eyed up the steam shower with multiple heads and moaned. "Oh, I'm going to enjoy using that."

Pete cleared his throat. "Right, uh...um...make yourself at home. The towels on the rack are clean." He glanced at her, then back at the shower. "I'll um...I'll let you get settled."

"Uh-uh, I want to see your room," she replied.

Pete groaned. "Sure."

"What's the groan about?" she asked.

"Nothing. I didn't groan."

"Yeah, you did."

"Jesus, Ken, drop it, please."

She stepped closer to him, and he stepped back. "Do I make you uncomfortable, Pete?" she asked.

"What? No, of course not."

Interesting. Then why did he look like he wanted to flee? She took another step toward him. His eyes darkened as he held her stare. "You sure?" she whispered.

"Be careful, Kendall."

"Of what?"

"What you're asking for," he replied. His nostrils flared as he watched her.

She placed her hand against his muscular chest. "What am I asking for?" she licked her lips as she held his stare.

"Fuck," he muttered and stepped away from her. "That's a bad idea, Kendall, and you know it."

"Why is it a bad idea?"

"Because your brother would kill me," Pete protested.

"No, he wouldn't. You guys are friends. He likes you."

Pete rolled his eyes. "There's a big difference between liking me as a buddy and liking me enough to let me touch his sister. Ryan doesn't like anyone that much."

"Well then, it's a good thing my brother doesn't get to decide who I fuck."

"Jesus," Pete groaned.

"In case you hadn't noticed. I'm all grown-up, Pete."

"Believe me, I noticed," he grumbled.

"So, what's the problem?" she asked and stepped toward him again. "We're obviously attracted to each other. We're both healthy, single adults. What's the harm in having a little fun while I'm here?"

"Again, your brother is one of my best friends and he'd kill me if I took advantage of you while you're staying with me."

"Oh my god, did you seriously just say that?" Kendall scoffed. "Take advantage of me, because the poor little lady couldn't possibly know her own mind." She poked him in the chest. "Believe me, Pete. I know my own mind and if I fuck a guy, it's because I want to fuck him. Not because I'm so naïve he's tricked me into it."

He caught her hand as she continued to poke his chest. "I didn't mean it like that," he growled. "There's just like a code that you don't cross. You don't fuck your friend's ex, and you sure as hell keep your hands off his sister."

"But what if the sister wants you to put your hands on her?" She leaned in so their bodies were touching and he sucked in a breath.

"Still, he'd kill me if he found out."

"So maybe he doesn't need to find out," she whispered as she leaned in closer and shifted her hips. She could feel him getting hard against her stomach. He was definitely not immune to her. "I'm only here for a week, Pete. My brother is out of town. You and I barely ever see each other." She leaned in and whispered in his ear. "No one would ever have to know."

His hand curled around her hip and she bit back a smile. Not wanting to press her luck, she stepped back. "Think about it," she said and turned and walked out of the bathroom.

His body tensed like a caged animal and he looked around the room. "We should head back downstairs," he said.

"Sure."

Pete started to push past her. When his chest brushed against her shoulder, he stopped, muttered something unintelligible, and gestured for her to go first. Kendall bit back a smile. It was like he was scared to touch her. Maybe this would be easier than she thought.

CHAPTER TWO

Pete reached into the fridge and pulled out a couple of bottles of water. He slid one across the island toward Kendall.

Shit, even the kitchen wasn't big enough. Who knew she'd grown up to be so hot? She'd always been attractive, but the woman standing in front of him was a freaking knockout. When had Ryan's little sister become this sexy woman? *This was not good.*

When he'd said yes to letting her stay with him, he'd been thinking of teenaged Kendall, cute but awkward. Not someone he'd be tempted to break bro-code over. But this Kendall was a whole other story. As if they had a mind of their own his eyes trailed down her body, lingering on the exposed swatch of skin where her shirt pulled up as she leaned against the counter, exposing her smooth flat stomach.

He needed to do something to get them outside and away from all the surfaces his mind was busy picturing her spread out on. The island had never looked better to him. He cleared his throat.

"You still like to hike?" he asked.

"Yeah, love it."

"Did you bring something you can walk in?"

Kendall rolled her eyes. "Um, come on Pete, of course I brought something I can walk in. I brought all my workout stuff with me. How hard a hike are we talking? Do I need to change or just grab runners?"

"I thought we'd just do Torrey Pines. It's pretty easy, but has amazing views and will get us out of the house."

Kendall flashed him an amused smile. "Well, by all means, let's go get some fresh air. Let me just grab my shoes." She turned and jogged up the stairs towards the bedroom.

When she disappeared from view, he realized he'd been watching her the entire time. Crap. He needed to get it together. As sexy as Kendall was, she was Ryan's sister. He'd asked him to watch over her while she was in town. That sure as hell didn't include watching her naked. Shit, now he really wanted to see her naked. He dropped his head back and looked up at the ceiling and took a deep, cleansing breath.

Shaking off the images of Kendall naked, he grabbed a backpack off the hook by the front door and threw their water bottles inside. He dropped onto the bench and slid his feet into sneakers. At the sound of Kendall descending the stairs, he glanced up and sucked in a breath. She'd tied her hair up into a high ponytail, and he could just picture pulling out the elastic and watching her caramel brown hair tumble around her shoulders. Keeping his hands to himself this week was going to be a lot harder than he'd ever imagined.

Kendall walked up to him and wrapped her arms around him, pulling him into another hug. "It's really great to see you again. Thanks for taking the time to hang out and show me around. I've missed hiking and doing all that outdoorsy stuff."

At the feel of her body against him, his dick instantly joined the party. *So not cool.* He gave her a stiff hug and stepped back. This was Ryan's little sister. She's off limits. He mentally chastised himself.

Annoyed with his body's response, he clenched his jaw. What the hell was wrong with him? Grabbing the keys out of the bowl, he pulled open the front door. "All right, let's go," he muttered.

He wandered over to his Range Rover and double clicked the key fob to unlock the doors.

"Nice," Kendall said as she pulled open the door. "I've always really liked these cars." She ran her hand along the seat and sighed. Pete's dick twitched at the sound as he watched her stroking the buttery soft leather.

"Don't you just want to wrap yourself in this leather?" she asked.

"Uh...um, never really thought about it." He'd like to wrap something around her all right. God, he was an asshole. Not everything she said needed to be taken sexually. He watched her as she clicked her seatbelt, then stroked the leather again. His fingers clenched around the steering wheel. Tell that to his dick.

Throwing the car in reverse, he hit the gas and peeled out of the stall. The faster he got to where they were going, the faster he could get out of this confined space with Kendall.

"Do you mind?" she asked as she touched the knob for the stereo.

"Not at all," he muttered.

Kendall scrolled through the stations until she found something she liked. She leaned her head back against the seat and faced him, her fingers still trailing along the seat.

"Can you please stop stroking the goddamn seat," he growled.

Kendall winced and pulled her hands into her lap. "Sorry."

"Shit, no I'm sorry." He exhaled audibly. "You just got me a little amped up with the sex talk and then the stroking and—" He paused. "Yeah, uh... not to be a dick, I'm just trying really hard not to think about you like that and it's a little hard when you keep rubbing the chair and making those little noises."

"I'm not making noises," she gasped.

"Yeah, you are. And it's driving me fucking crazy, so can you just—"

She clasped her hands tightly together like she'd been chastised at school. God, he was a grown-ass man. He should be able to be alone in a car with a beautiful woman and not be ruled by his hormones.

"Sorry." She turned her head and looked at him again. "I'm not going to lie and say I'm sorry you're attracted to me, but I'm sorry if you are feeling pressured. I would never want to do that to you."

"I'm not feeling pressured," he grumbled.

Kendall's soft laughter filled the car and some of the tension eased from his body.

"So, tell me about where we're going?"

"Torrey Pines, it's not a hard hike at all, but I think you'll like it." He checked over his shoulder, then changed lanes. "The path walks along the bluffs and overlooks the water. With the breeze off the ocean, and the birds, it's always really nice, peaceful, even when it's busy, which it shouldn't be too bad today."

"Sounds perfect."

"How are the folks?

"Eh, same ol' same ol'. They're happy Ryan was traded to this side of the country so they can see their baby boy more often."

"Good for them, kind of shitty for you, hey?"

"It won't make too much of a difference for me, I don't think, other than in the offseason. We didn't really see each other very much when he was playing. At least now he'll play in Atlanta, so I'll get to see him when you have games in town."

"Oh yeah, decisions, decisions. Do you cheer for the home team or big brother?"

"My loyalties will be torn for sure, but seeing how Ryan wouldn't have made it to the Bigs if he hadn't been whipping balls at my head when we were kids, I should probably cheer for him."

"You played catch with him?"

"Sure. I played softball growing up, so we practiced a lot together when we were young."

"I didn't know you played softball."

"Yep, DIV1 scholarship and everything."

"Seriously? You were that good? Why did I not know this about you?"

She shrugged. "DIV1 girls' softball doesn't exactly hold a candle to a major league contract."

"I don't know. That's still pretty freaking impressive."

"Mmm," she mumbled something that sounded like, "Tell that to my parents."

"I'll bet your parents were pretty happy that both you and Ry got free rides to school. They must be really proud of you both."

"Yeah, mom and dad are ridiculously proud of Ryan. I don't think they meet anyone who doesn't quickly find out about their major league son."

"They must brag about you a lot too. God, if I'd gone to college my mom would have been over the moon. I think she would have bragged about that more than she ever brags about my baseball."

"How's your mom doing?"

"She's doing good. She's looking forward to coming down for a visit in the summer."

"That's nice that she's coming for a visit," Kendall replied.

"Yeah, do your folks ever make it to Atlanta?"

"No."

"Never?"

"Nope, they've never been.

"Seriously? I thought they went to Florida last year for Ryan's training camp."

"Yep, they did." Kendall shifted in her seat and flicked the radio dial to a new station.

"And they didn't stop and see you?"

"No, I went down to Florida for a few days and saw them."

"Huh." He couldn't imagine his mom coming that close and not stopping in to see where he lived. He knew Ryan's parents were coming to town to see his new place later in the summer. It was strange they hadn't gone to see Kendall's. "What do they think of your fancy job?"

"I wouldn't call it fancy," she replied. "But they're happy I can support myself and don't need money." She turned and looked out the window without elaborating any further. He waited for her to say something, but she just continued to look out the window.

"Say hi next time you're talking to them." He thought back to all the times he'd been at their house and how welcoming they always were. That hadn't always been the case with his friends growing up. "Your parents were always really good to me."

"Of course," she murmured while still looking out the window.

Pete flicked a glance at her, curious why she was so quiet. He replayed over their conversation, but there was nothing they'd talked about that should have changed the mood in the vehicle that much. This was why he didn't ever lock himself in to having a girlfriend. Women were way too confusing. Kendall had gone from vampy to sad all in the span of a twenty-minute car ride.

He pulled the car into the parking lot and turned off the car.

Kendall sat forward in her seat. "Wow, if it's this pretty from the parking lot, I can't wait to go see what else there is." She flashed him a huge smile and threw open the car door.

And now she seemed back to normal. Whatever had momentarily shifted the mood in the car was gone. The woman was a mystery.

He scooped up the backpack and slid it over his shoulders. "Let's hit it," he called as he walked towards the trail.

Kendall fell into step beside him as he wove past a few people who were wrapping up their walk.

"How do you like San Diego now that you've been here for a few years?" Kendall asked.

"I love it. I could quite easily stay here forever."

"Really?"

"Yeah, it has everything I want. Warm weather, the ocean, good hikes, good ball."

A couple of women in spandex shorts and sports bras jogged past, and Kendall grinned over at him. "Scantily clad women," she teased.

Pete raised his arms. "There is that. I mean, what are you gonna do, right?"

Kendall snickered. "So many women, so little time."

"Something like that," he joked. "What's your dating life like back in Atlanta?"

"It's there. Nothing to write home about."

"I thought you were pretty serious about a guy a while back."

"I wouldn't say I was serious. We dated for a while." She kicked a loose rock off the path, then another before finally speaking. "I think we dated as long as we did because it was easy. We both liked the same things. It was fun to have someone to catch a game with, that kind of thing, since most of my friends don't really watch sports."

"Catch a game, have a couple dogs, wrap it up with sex. Every guy's dream date," he teased.

"Something like that. Except we often skipped the sex part."

"What? That's the best part of the evening. Why the hell would you skip the sex?" What man in his right mind would skip sex with Kendall at the end of the evening? What was the point of having a relationship if you weren't going to have sex?

"Thus the breakup." She flicked a glance over at him. "I kind of think maybe we both enjoyed watching the guys in the tight pants more than the sex with each other."

Pete snorted. "He was gay?"

"Not exclusively, obviously, since we dated for a year, but he was pretty fluid in who he was attracted to."

"Huh." He walked beside her silently for several minutes. Unable to help himself, he asked, "What about the guys you're dating now?"

"Honestly, the last few guys I've dated have been duds. The guys who don't like sports really don't enjoy watching sports, and I love them, so that's out. And the last guy I went out with, we went to a basketball game and..." She paused. "I don't know how to describe him other than to say he's one of those guys who would have his chest painted with a letter if he was at the game with his boys." She scrunched up her face as she glanced at him. "I mean, I like sports as much as the next person, but that's a bit much, even for me."

"Dating's rough," Pete replied.

Kendall snorted. "Yeah, I'm sure dating is really tough for the mighty Pete Saunders."

"What's that mean?"

"I don't know. Women throw themselves at you all the time. You probably have to beat them off with a stick. Exhibit A," she said, gesturing to herself.

"You didn't throw yourself at me." How the hell did they get back to talking about them hooking up?

"It was damn close," she scoffed.

He glanced over at Kendall and she looked almost hurt. Shit.

"Dating sucks," he said, trying to get them back on even ground and away from them.

"Yeah, and it doesn't help that I don't know...I'm more like a guy than a girl when it comes to sex."

Don't say it. "Why's that?" Shit, he wasn't supposed to ask.

"I don't know, maybe because I grew up around sports, the whole nudity and sex thing is often so casual in that environment, so I just don't see what the big deal is. I find the whole dating thing a bit awkward and I mean I'm a girl—if I want sex I can find someone who will have sex with me. I don't need to bother with the whole painful getting to know you part." She grimaced. "Hell, if I actually got to know most of the guys I hooked up with, there was no way I would have had sex with them." She glanced over at him and grimaced. "And now you think I'm a slut."

Pete went to speak, and the words got stuck. He cleared his throat. "I don't think you're a slut."

"What do you think?"

Abort. Abort. They needed to change the subject immediately. He was no saint and if Kendall kept suggesting how open she was to hooking up, he was going to take her up on the offer. Despite what a bad idea it would be.

"I think we need to change the subject." He walked down to the beach and kicked off his shoes. "Let's walk on the beach."

"Chicken," she teased.

"Absolutely," he replied, and he wasn't even ashamed to admit it.

Back at his place, he hung up the backpack and walked towards the living room. Kendall dropped down on the couch beside him. She rested her back against the arm of the couch and curled her feet up on the seat beside her so she was facing him.

"That was a lot of fun. Thanks for taking me."

"No problem. Glad you enjoyed it."

Kendall closed her eyes and dropped her head back, rolling her neck back and forth. She dug her finger into the base of her skull and moaned.

Christ, why did she have to make so many sexy little noises? Was she doing it on purpose to drive him crazy, or was she just inherently that sexy?

"Headache?" he asked.

"Not really, just a tight neck. I don't know why flying always makes me stiff. I'm glad we were able to go hiking. That helped a lot."

She pushed her fingers up the back of her head and made a little growly noise that had him smiling. Hooking her fingers in her elastic, she pulled.

His mouth dropped open as he watched her hair tumble down her back. That was so much sexier in real life than what he had pictured. Crap, they'd been back in the house for all of ten minutes and he was hard again and picturing her naked.

"I need a drink," Pete muttered.

Kendall's eyes popped open. "Sounds good. Why don't we go grab some dinner somewhere?"

"K, let's go," he said as he hopped off the couch. Bending down, he grabbed her hand and pulled her up so they could leave before all his good intentions went out the door.

"You okay with pub food?" Pete asked as they walked out the front door of his place.

"Sounds good."

"There's a place at the end of the pier that is pretty good." They began walking side by side down the pier. "It's a brewpub with the brewery next door. It's pretty cool. It started as just this little micro-brewery, then over the past few years they've grown and become so popular they took over the old factory next door."

"What made you buy down here?" Kendall asked.

"I don't know. I've always wanted to be by the water but I don't...I don't really fit with the people who can afford to live there normally in a city like this." His friends all thought he was crazy to want to live in a converted warehouse along the water. Converting the old printing press warehouse into three 4,000 sq ft homes had been a gigantic labor of love. But it turned out better than he'd ever imagined. Sure, it wasn't the most convenient location, but he loved it.

"What do you mean? Why wouldn't you fit in with them?"

He could feel Kendall looking at him as they walked. "I just didn't grow up like that and it doesn't feel like me."

He glanced over at her, and she was giving him a weird look. "Don't get me wrong, places like Ryan bought are great and I can totally see the appeal. It's just not the right fit for me personally."

Kendall laughed. "You don't have to explain yourself to me. I love your place. I much prefer it to what I imagine my brother bought. It just surprised me, that's all."

"Why's that?"

"I don't know. Growing up, you seemed kind of flashy and always loved lots of attention and I guess I thought you'd want the big fancy house everyone would admire."

He winced. "God, I wasn't that much of a prick, was I?"

She stopped walking and gawked at him. "What? You weren't a prick."

"No? Just all flash and no substance." He cringed. He knew he'd had a pretty big ego when he was younger and was kind of full of himself when he first got signed, but hearing Kendall's impression of him stung a little.

"I never said that." Kendall grabbed his arm. "You had something to prove to the world. I got that. It didn't make you a prick. It made you hungry. Determined. You had a bit of a chip on your shoulder when I first met you, but it was more of a screw you. No one is going to tell me what I can and can't do."

If only she knew how true that was. Before his dad had left, he'd taken every opportunity to tell Pete what a useless piece of shit he was. How much he regretted him being born. He'd always felt like he was a big part of the reason his dad had left. When things started to look up for him with baseball, his biggest dream had been to finally prove his old man wrong.

Kendall's hand brushed against his arm, drawing his attention back to her. She smiled at him and began walking again. "You had this whole bad boy vibe going. It was pretty hot."

"Oh yeah?" He flicked a glance at her, then pulled open the door to the restaurant.

The hostess smiled. "Hey, Pete. For two?"

"Yeah, thanks, Carla."

They followed Carla to a table against the window that overlooked the water.

Kendall slid into her seat and looked around the restaurant. "I like it, it's trendy without being cheugy."

"Chew gee? What the fuck is that?"

Kendall rolled her eyes. "You know, like trying too hard."

Pete snorted. "You just made that up. There's no way that's a real word."

"It totally is a word." She placed her hand against her chest. "I'm offended you think I'd lie about something like that."

"Must be some bougie Atlanta term because I've never heard it before."

"Well, you know." She flicked her hair off her shoulder. "I am in marketing, after all, so I have to keep up to date on what all the cool kids are saying." She stuck her tongue out and smirked.

"Oh right, of course. I just didn't realize I wasn't still a cool kid." Shit, he'd just turned thirty. How was that old?

Kendall reached across the table and squeezed his hand. "Don't worry, you're still cool to me."

"Gee, thanks."

The server stopped at their table. "Can I bring you something to drink?"

Kendall glanced over at the bar and quirked her brow as she pondered the selection. "Sorry, I don't know what kind of beer you have."

"But you want beer?"

"Come on, Pete. I would be kicked out of the Graves family if I didn't drink beer."

He pictured Ryan's dad and all the attempts at making beer in the basement he'd made over the past decade. He shuddered. God, some of them had been horrific. Some things should be left for the professionals or at least people who had a better understanding of science than Pat. "I'm sure we can do better than your dad's basement beer." He laughed, then turned to the server. "Can we grab two samplers and just load it up with your 10 best sellers and we can split it to figure out what we like?"

"I don't go to brew pubs very often at home, so I forgot they do that. Fun." She leaned back in her chair. "Thanks for letting me crash with you. I really appreciate it."

"No problem. I'm glad you asked. It'll be nice to spend some time with you. We've never really hung out, just the two of us before."

"Yeah, it'll be nice to get to know each other better as adults." She smiled at him.

And instantly, his cock was back at the party. Son of a bitch. The thing had a mind of its own around her. He was going to have to put a leash on the damn thing if this kept up. She was here for work. She didn't need her brother's friend lusting after her.

"Advertising huh, what's that like?"

The look on Kendall's face said she knew exactly what he was doing with the little dodge and weave game he was playing as he tried to avoid anything that might steer them back towards discussing hooking up. With any other woman, he would be all over a casual fling and enjoying the hell out of the week, but this was Ryan's sister and he could almost hear him warning Pete off her as they spoke.

"Advertising is good. I work at a boutique firm in Atlanta that recently opened an office here in San Diego."

"You've worked there, what, five years?"

"Yeah, I started there right out of University. I did an internship with the firm my summer before graduating and it was like a dream come true when they hired me after graduation."

"Why's that? What's special about the firm?"

"I don't know, it's just..." She shook her head and paused, like she was trying to find the words to explain it. "The company was started by these four amazing women. They were only a few years older than me when they started the firm with some startup money from a couple of investors who now live in San Diego, thus the new office here." Her eyes glittered with excitement when she looked back at him. "They are absolutely incredible and so creative. Somehow they're able to convince these stodgy business men to try innovative ad campaigns that no one would ever expect them to be willing to try. I've learned so much from them."

"That's awesome. You were lucky to hook up with them right out of the gate."

"Oh, tell me about it. They took me under their wing right away and have even helped me with taking some advanced business courses to learn that aspect of the company as well. It's been pretty wild."

Her voice hummed with excitement as she spoke about her job. If she could be that passionate about work, he could only imagine what she'd be like in bed. Woah. He needed to rein those kind of thoughts in and fast. He was not going to think about her like that. She was Ryan's sister. Ryan's kid sister. He'd known her since before puberty had really kicked in. He would not think about her as a woman.

He glanced across the table, and Kendall smiled at him. Ok, that might be easier said than done. Why the hell did she have to grow up to look like that?

Smart, beautiful, and liked baseball. That was like the freaking trifecta. Ok, he needed to get his thoughts back on track. Talk about work. Most people were willing to talk about themselves to the point of being annoying about it. That ought to curb his lust for her.

"Why'd they send you here to San Diego?"

"Mmm, they just started the firm about six months ago and thought the person they hired would be a perfect fit. He seemed to have the same philosophy as them, but somehow that doesn't seem to translate with clients. All four of my bosses are married with young kids and it's not convenient for them to come out here just to get the lay of the land. I'm here to see what's going on, get a feel for things and then, if need be, one of them will come out and make some changes. None of them will ever move here, so if it turns out it's going to be too hard to get this up and running properly, they may just decide to sell." She shrugged. "We'll see. It's still too soon to tell. At this point, we don't know if it's a management issue, a staffing issue or something else. So that's what I'll be doing this week while I'm here. Playing detective and putting my new business management classes to good use."

She placed her elbows on the table and leaned towards him. "Okay, enough about me. You must be pretty excited that Ryan got traded to San Diego so you two can play together again."

What? They couldn't be done talking about her already. No woman was willing to jump to talking about him that quickly. He'd been counting on her boring him with shop talk to cool down the lust that sizzled beneath the surface since the second he laid eyes on her again.

He scanned the bar for their server. Where the hell were their drinks?

CHAPTER THREE

The server stopped at the table with two trays of beer samplers. She laid a piece of paper on the table beside each tray. "This lists the beers in each sampler with a score sheet for you to rate which ones you like best. Are you wanting to order now as well, or do you need more time?"

He looked over at Kendall, and she glanced at the menu she hadn't opened yet and winced. "Yeah, we're going to need more time," he told her.

"No problem. Just give me a wave when you want to order."

Kendall picked up the sheet in front of her and slid a tray toward herself. He'd never seen anyone take beer tasting so seriously before. She studied the beers, looked back at her list, then swooped in and scooped up the list in front of him.

"Hey, that one's mine." He grabbed her hand to try to get the sheet back.

She sucked in a breath when their hands touched. Raising his head, he looked at her and held her gaze for several seconds. The air hummed between them.

Her voice shook slightly when she spoke. "I thought we were going to share."

"I don't share well with others." Shit, why did he say it like that? They were talking about beer and he made it sound like he was a possessive caveman who didn't share his woman. Which was a lie because he'd been known to do that too. The sheet dropped to the table and he let go of Kendall's hand. What was wrong with him? He prided himself on always being cool. He didn't get weird about women.

"Are we just going to dance around this sexual tension for the entire week, then?" Kendall pinned him with a look. And damn if that didn't make her even hotter that she was confident enough to call him on his bullshit.

"I thought we agreed it was a bad idea for anything to happen between us."

"No, you said it was a bad idea. I disagreed. I think it sounds like a fantastic idea."

Pete shifted in his seat and his dick twitched beneath his fly, letting him know it thought it was a great idea as well.

"Do you know how many times your brother warned me off you when we were kids?"

"We aren't kids anymore, Pete."

"No, I know, but still Ryan has made it clear he doesn't want his friends touching his sister."

"And yet he was the one who suggested I call you and stay with you instead of getting a hotel."

Yeah, what was that all about? It's not like her work wouldn't pay for a hotel, so why had Ryan pushed her to call him? "He probably figured you were safe with me."

"There's safe and then there's safe, Pete." Kendall picked up her necklace and moved the charm back and forth on the chain like a seductive pendulum. When she stopped in the middle of her chest, his eyes lingered on her cleavage, and that twitch became a throb. Shit, he was in trouble.

"I'm not the teenage girl you remember."

"Believe me, I'm very well aware." The girl he remembered was shy and a little bit awkward. The woman in front of him was anything but. She dropped her necklace and it landed between her breasts. Unable to stop himself, his eyes lingered on the skin where the necklace landed. This woman knew her appeal and was willing to use it to her advantage.

Kendall slid the beer scoring sheet towards her and flipped it over, drew a line down the middle, and began writing.

"What are you writing?"

"A pros and cons list." She winked at him. "I seem to remember you doing them when we were kids."

"Pros and cons to us sleeping together?" he asked, amused at the effort she was willing to go to convince him this was a good idea.

"Yep, I told you I'll pull out all the stops on this one." Kendall pulled her bottom lip between her teeth and smiled coyly, then wrote on the sheet.

Finally, she slid the paper towards him. Holy shit, she was a dirty girl. She definitely made some fine points.

The only thing on the con list was Ryan. The pro side was completely filled and the woman made good points.

Maybe she was onto something, and he should at least hear her out. It's not like he had to follow through with anything, but she was right. She was an adult and deserved the chance to plead her case.

"Didn't you grow up in Vegas?" Kendall asked.

"Yeah, why?" Where was she going with this? He leaned back in his chair and looked her in the eye. A small, sly smile spread across her face.

"Well, I'm thinking this week can be like Vegas. What happens here stays here."

He shook his head. "This isn't Vegas, Ken."

"No, but it can be like it if we want it to be." She leaned forward and clasped her hands together beneath her chin. The movement pressed her breast together and he bit back a groan.

"I'm only here for a week. Ryan is already at training camp, so there's zero chance of us seeing him." She licked her lips slowly. "You can't deny the chemistry between us. I know I'm going to be spending the entire week thinking about you either way, and I'll be doing my best to convince you we should fuck."

He shifted on the stool and pulled on the corner pocket of his jeans to subtly shift the fabric in an effort to ease the tightness.

"I can be very persuasive, Pete. I convince people they want things for a living and believe me, I am very good at my job."

"Yeah, I can tell."

"I'm thinking it makes more sense to enjoy the entire week and get the most out of it rather than both of us being sexually frustrated all week long until we get to the point where we finally cave the night before I leave in a feast of sweaty, carnal lust. I mean, I'm all for that too, but I think it would be more fun to partake all week."

"Okay, but are you going to be able to make it just about sex this week? I don't want you to weave fairytales around this becoming something. Because I promise you, it won't," Pete told her.

"Believe me, I'm very well aware of your reputation, Pete. I have no illusions about what this is."

"Are you sure? Because I'd be lying if I said I wasn't tempted, but no offense, I can't fuck up my friendship with Ryan because you want it to become something more. I'm sorry if that makes me sound like an asshole."

"No, it honestly doesn't. I don't want to have to deal with shit from my brother any more than you do."

"What does that mean?"

"Oh, come on. Exactly what you're worried about, but on the other side. He'd lecture me about how stupid I was to get involved with you. You're a pro-athlete. You aren't going to end up with a girl like me, blah blah blah."

"What the fuck? Why wouldn't I end up with a girl like you?" He knew Kendall was too good for him, but that didn't mean he would end up with some groupie. Hell, he'd long since outgrown the novelty of that.

Kendall rolled her eyes. "It's not a shot at you, it's a shot at me."

"From where I'm sitting, there is absolutely nothing wrong with you."

"Well, thank you." She tilted her head to the side as she watched him. "So, I propose we take advantage of the forced proximity this week to bang the hell out of each other. Then when I go home, we go back to business as usual."

"How would that work when we see each other?"

"Come on, Pete, how often is that going to happen? In the past five years, how many times have we seen each other? Two, maybe three?"

"Yeah, but that will be different now that Ryan's been traded to the same team as me."

"Not really. I might see you when you guys come to Atlanta for a game, but Ryan will be there, so it's not like anything would happen anyway, so it would just be like normal."

"And you think you can be normal with me after we've had sex?"

Kendall leaned back in her chair and laughed. "Umm yeah, I think I can be normal around you after we've had sex. I might live in the south, but I'm not some pearl clutching virgin who's going to be all scandalized because you took my honor," she said, her voice dripping with a false southern accent. "Trust me, I can be cool around my brother if you can."

Damn, she made a good point. Could he do this? Could he hook up with Kendall with no strings? His head said, don't be an asshole. She deserved better than a casual hookup with a guy like him. His dick said he was being an asshole if he didn't take her seriously and respect that she knew her own mind. Problem was, he didn't know which head to listen to. He picked up one of the beers from the tray without even looking at the list and took a sip.

Kendall reached out and took the beer from his hand and brought the glass to her mouth for a sip. She handed the glass back to him when she'd finished. He looked down at the glass and the faint lipstick mark on the rim from where her lips had rested. How messed up was it that he wanted to place his lips over that lipstick stain?

"I can be cool around your brother. But if we do this, no one finds out."

Kendall held his gaze. "And when I leave, we go back to the way things have always been. No feeling guilty and trying to drag this thing out because you're scared of hurting my feelings. We fuck, get it out of our systems and go back to normal."

Pete took a deep breath and exhaled. Hopefully, they wouldn't regret this decision, but at this particular moment, he didn't care. "Deal," he agreed. *Looks like my little brain won this round.*

"Let's get out of here," Kendall said.

"You don't want to eat first?" he asked. God, he hoped not because now that they'd agreed to do this, he couldn't wait to get back home.

"Not even a little bit. We can order pizza or something later."

"Done." He threw a twenty on the table and stood up. Reaching for her hand, he pulled her out of her chair. She pressed against him and grabbed his belt buckle with her fingers.

"No changing your mind, no feeling guilty, no regrets. Deal?"

"Deal." Now he just hoped he could live with his decision. Right or wrong, there was no way he wasn't taking Kendall up on what she'd offered. She was right. She was a grownup and could make her own decisions about her sex life. That didn't mean her brother would agree. Now he just had to make sure Ryan never found out.

As he watched Kendall walk towards the front door of the bar, a wave of lust unlike anything he'd ever felt surged through him. Fuck it, he'd deal with the consequences if Ryan found out.

CHAPTER FOUR

The air crackled with sexual tension as they walked down the pier towards Pete's house. The entire meal felt like foreplay. Kendall was conscious of exactly how turned on she was already. Her nipples pressed against her bra, the tightness almost painful against the lace. God, she hoped Pete wasn't just a big tease and he planned to follow through on all the heated looks he'd been giving her at the pub. She glanced over at him, taking note of his clenched jaw as he walked. Her gaze flicked down to his jeans. Damn, in this light, she couldn't tell if he was aroused or not.

God, the tension was killing her. Why was he walking so slow? She wanted to race him back to his place so she could jump on him, and he was taking this leisurely stroll. Maybe she'd misread things.

He was a professional ballplayer. Women threw themselves at him all the time and from what her brother had told her, the guys weren't exactly discerning. They'd pretty much take whatever was offered. Kind of like being offered a bowl of vanilla ice-cream. People ate it because it was ice cream, but it wasn't something they couldn't live without. She chewed her bottom lip. *Oh god. Was she vanilla ice-cream?*

Sure, she'd had sex, but she wasn't exactly the most experienced person in the art of seduction. Certainly not on par with a professional athlete.

Pete threaded his hand through hers as they walked. "Relax, Peanut, you're stressing me out."

She glanced over at him. "Sorry," she said and squeezed his hand.

"Nothing has to happen tonight."

"Oh no, it's happening, believe me," she told him.

Pete held her stare as they walked. "Good." He licked his lips. "We're in agreement then, casual, no strings, hot, secret sex."

She nodded in agreement. "I'm definitely in for some hot, secret sex." She'd wanted Pete since she was twelve years old and saw him for the first time. Temporary or not, she'd take him anyway she could get him. Maybe then she'd get this ridiculous crush out of her system. She'd go months without thinking of him, but then she'd hear his name or see his face on TV and wham, there it was.

Pathetic, really. Maybe he'd suck in bed and everything she'd built up would be for nothing. She looked over at him and he smiled. Yeah, there was no way he sucked in bed.

At his front door, Pete eased the key into the door and stepped back to allow her to precede him into the loft.

The second the door snicked shut, he was on her. Strong arms banded around her waist from behind and his hot mouth bit down on her neck. "Jesus, you've been driving me nuts all night," he admitted.

He spun her around and pressed her against the wall. His touch was hungry and urgent as he pushed his knee between her legs. "This is such a bad idea, but I don't seem to be able to talk myself out of it," he told her.

"Good." She tilted her head to give him better access and his tongue trailed up her neck to her earlobe. Holy shit. Pete Saunders was licking her.

She threaded her hands through his hair and pulled his face towards her. Their lips collided, and he pressed his tongue between her lips. There was nothing shy or unsure about his kiss. This was the kiss of a man who knew what he was doing. His thigh rubbed between her legs as his tongue thrust into her mouth. She couldn't get close enough to him. She gyrated her hips against his leg, needing to release some of the tension building in her core.

He grabbed her hips and hoisted her up. Yes, this was what she'd been waiting for. She wrapped her legs around his waist as he carried her toward the staircase.

Pete broke the kiss and gripped her hips with his hands. "You gotta stop doing that or I'm going to fuck you here on the stairs and it really won't be my best work."

"This isn't supposed to be a job, Pete," she said, before taking his earlobe into her mouth.

He groaned when she pulled the lobe with her teeth. "Well, you know anything worth doing is worth doing well. I might not be the first guy you've fucked, Ken, but I'm going to be the most memorable."

Her chest tightened at his words. True, but not necessarily for the reasons, he thought.

He walked into his bedroom and set her down on the floor. His hands immediately reached for the bottom of her shirt and lifted it over her head. Stepping back, he paused and looked at her. His tongue slowly ran along his bottom lip as his heated stare ran down her body. He bit down on his bottom lip and his eyes darkened even further. Kendall shivered with anticipation and looked down at herself. Oh god, if she'd known she was going to get naked with Pete today, she would have worn different underwear.

He flicked the little bow in the center of her bra. "Cute, I wouldn't have figured you for a polka dots girl."

God, she was trying to show him what a confident woman she'd become, and he caught her wearing a teenage girl's bra.

Trying for a bravado she didn't particularly feel, she pressed her chest out, putting her breasts on display. "Polka dots can be sexy too."

Pete traced his finger along the top edge of her bra, following the line all the way across one breast, then the other. "I'm pretty sure anything would look sexy on you." He continued to trace his finger down her breast, somehow homing in on her nipple even through the padded fabric. "If I'd known you looked like this when we were kids, I don't think anything Ryan said would have kept me away from you."

"It's probably best you didn't see me then," she replied.

God lord, if he'd known what she'd looked like as a teen, he would have run the other way. She'd been late to the developmental party and barely had anything that resembled breasts before she was eighteen, then practically developed overnight. There was no way teenaged Pete would have looked twice at her in her underwear.

"Probably." He flicked the clasp of her bra open with one hand. She gulped. Shit, he was a lot more practiced at this than she'd thought. *Oh boy.*

He dropped her bra down onto the floor. Stepping back, he looked at her. "Fuck," he said. The gritty sound of need in his voice had moisture pooling in her core.

"You need to lose your shirt too," she told him.

He raised an eyebrow at her. "That right?"

"Mmm hmm. Fair's fair, you got to see me, I should get to see you."

He peeled his shirt over his head and tossed it on the floor. Her tongue stuck to the roof of her mouth and an embarrassingly unintelligible sound slid out of her throat as she took in the muscular chest in front of her. She'd expected him to have a good body, but this was ridiculous.

When she finally peeled her eyes off his chest and looked at him, Pete stood watching her with a crooked smirk on his face. "You all good?" he asked.

"Your muscles have muscles. That's insane."

Pete dipped his head like he was embarrassed by her assessment and her heart squeezed a little tighter. God, he wasn't supposed to be all shy and sweet. He was supposed to just be a wham bam kind of guy.

Needing to get her mind back in control, she stepped towards him and hooked her hand in the waistband of his jeans. She eyed the wolf tattoo that covered his shoulder and upper arm. "Wow, this beautiful," she said, trailing her finger along the head of the wolf.

"Thanks." Pete brushed her hair off her shoulder and sucked her earlobe into his mouth.

"Why a wolf?" she asked.

"Seriously?" he chuckled and rested his forehead against the top of her head.

Kendall giggled at the tortured sound of his voice. "You can pause for a second."

"I don't know if that's true," he complained, then sighed. "It's Fenrir."

"It's what?"

"Fenrir, like from Norse mythology." Pete raked his hands through his hair, making it stand up like he's just rolled out of bed. Mmm, she could just imagine how good he would look fresh out of bed in the morning.

"Why'd you pick him?" She slowly followed the intricate linework with the tip of her finger, enjoying the way Pete shivered beneath her touch.

He cleared his throat before speaking. "My mom is first generation American, her parents came over from Iceland, so I've always been pretty fascinated by Vikings and all that crap, thus Fenrir."

"Hmm, there feels like more to that story," Kendall murmured.

"Not tonight, there's not." Pete licked his lips as he stared down at her. Hunger radiated from him, making the man much like the wolf on his shoulder.

Without breaking eye contact, she undid the button at his waist and pushed his jeans down his muscular thighs.

Pete kicked his jeans off his feet and stood before her clad only in his black, tight boxer briefs. She sighed. "Your PR person should have you endorsing those," she murmured. Ads featuring Pete in his underwear would have sales soaring through the roof.

"Shut up," he mumbled, and her heart clenched again. God, she really needed to stop seeing this modest, sweet side of him or her plans to fuck him out of her system would morph into her falling in love with him, and that was not part of the program.

She dropped to her knees in front of him. "Ken," he warned.

"Mmm-hmm." She blinked up at him, loving the way his jaw clenched like he was hanging onto his control by a thread. Feeling powerful, she slid his underwear down his thighs, his muscles flexed beneath her touch. Sitting back on her knees, she licked her lips as she looked at his cock standing proudly out from his body, the bead of pre-come begging to be touched.

"You really don't have to," he said.

"I don't have to do anything, Pete." She grabbed his cock in her hand and swiped her tongue along the tip. The first taste of him hit her mouth and she bit back a moan. "I want to," she told him and sucked him deep into her mouth.

"Jesus," Pete groaned.

She slowly slid her mouth back over the tip and swirled her tongue around the little ridge beneath the head. Pete's fingers threaded through her hair, holding her in place. She bobbed up and down, reveling in the power of feeling Pete pliant beneath her touch. His fingers bit into her hair painfully as he fought for control, and she smiled around his cock. Before she even had a chance to glide down another time, he pulled back.

"Stop. The first time I come, I want it to be inside you," he growled.

Grabbing her arms, he pulled her off her knees. He clasped his hands around her waist and hoisted her up, forcing her to wrap her legs around him as he walked them toward the bed. He lay her down on the mattress and peeled her jeans and panties off her body. Her body thrummed with anticipation, making her skin feel hypersensitive. He trailed his hand up her inner thigh and she spread her legs wider. His finger dipped between her legs and he spread her moisture around her clit. "Jesus, you're soaked," he groaned.

Pete kneeled down on the mattress between her thighs. Bending, he took her nipple into his mouth as he continued to tease her clit with his hand. She squirmed beneath him. How could she be so close already? It was like her body had been waiting for this day its entire life. Pete dipped his finger inside her, then a second, and she arched her back off the bed. He sucked her nipple into his mouth, his teeth scraping against the bud, and she moaned.

Licking a path up her neck, he bit down on the pulse point in her throat, making a shiver course through her body. "You like that?" he asked as he flicked her clit.

"God, yes," she moaned.

Tension built inside her as her orgasm fought towards the surface. She gyrated her hips against his hand.

"Yeah, that's it. Fuck my fingers, Kendall." He curled his knuckle and her orgasm ripped through her. Oh my god. She bowed off the mattress, every muscle tightened as she came.

She collapsed back down and sighed. "Ok, that was..." She blew out a breath.

"Fucking hot?" Pete said.

"Yeah." She chuckled.

Looking him in the eye, his green eyes darkened to an almost moss color with lust rather than their normal lighter shade. She smiled and wrapped her hand around his cock.

"Hang on, let me grab a condom," he said, then leaned over to the bedside table and pulled out a sleeve and ripped one off.

Kneeling between her legs, he sheathed himself. He stared down at her, not moving, not saying anything. The air between them hummed with awareness. Finally, he shook his head like he was coming out of a fog and smiled. He leaned down and kissed her, slowly at first. The heat built as their tongues collided. She reached between them, grabbed his cock, and placed it at her entrance.

At the first thrust, she moaned. This was what she had been waiting for. She widened her legs to allow herself time to adjust to his size then ran her tongue up the side of his neck. He flashed her a sexy grin. "Hang on," he told her. The promise in his voice made an arrow of heat sizzle from her breasts to her clit. Lordy, this just got better and better.

He shifted his hips, angling deeper, and she wrapped her legs tighter around his waist. Normally first times with someone new were awkward, sometimes embarrassing, but she felt in sync with him, instinctively knowing how to match her body to his.

His fingers dug into her hips as he deepened the angle, driving them both higher and higher. Her heart pounded in her chest. She clasped her hands around his arms as there was nothing she could do but hang on as he took her body where he wanted it to go. The orgasm that screamed through her body seemed to come upon her out of nowhere, and her muscles clenched around him.

His body tensed above her as he came. "Fuck," Pete groaned.

Leaning down, he rested his head in the crook of her neck as they both gasped for breath. Ok, that wasn't supposed to happen. There was sex and then there was whatever that was.

"Holy shit," Pete uttered. "We are totally doing that again." He placed a kiss against her lips, then pushed himself off the bed and walked towards the ensuite to dispose of the condom.

Kendall dropped her arm over her eyes. And there was the difference between men and women. Here she was weaving fairytales about what their amazing sexual connection meant and all he was thinking about was going again.

She needed to remember that and protect her heart. This was supposed to be a casual week-long fling, and just because the sex was the stuff of romance novels didn't mean he would fall in love with her. *Don't fall in love. This is just sex. Freaking amazing sex, but still just sex.*

The mattress shifted beside her as Pete lay back down on the bed. Peeking her eyes open, she glanced over at him. He lay with his head propped on his elbow, looking at her. "You okay?" he asked.

"I'm great. You?"

"Yeah, I'm good too. Now I'm even more glad you talked me into this."

She rolled onto her side and narrowed her eyes at him. "Talked you into it?"

"Yeah, I mean, play the instant replay. There was some serious arm twisting involved," he teased.

Kendall reached out and twisted his nipple, laughing when he squealed. The sound was not something she ever would have expected to come out of Pete Saunders' mouth.

"Ouch," he laughed as he rubbed his nipple.

"You deserved it."

He shook his head. "You grew up mean, Peanut."

"You ain't seen nothing yet," she grumbled.

"I'm counting on it," Pete said. His eyes darkened with lust as he stared back at her.

Oh my. This was going to be a week she never forgot.

The following morning, she sat at the kitchen island and watched Pete making French toast.

"That is some stove," she said as she eyed the Viking gas range. "You obviously like to cook."

"Yeah, I love it. That's why the kitchen is the way it is. My mom worked as a cook and growing up, she was always complaining about our kitchen. When I got my first decent paycheck, the first thing I did was buy her a house." He shook his head. "It was like pulling teeth to get her to let me buy her something. It's a waste of good money. She had too many memories to move elsewhere," he pitched his voice higher, like he was imitating the way his mom spoke. He chuckled and rolled his eyes. "We ended up with this little house in my old neighborhood." He ran his hand down the side of his Viking range. "She did allow me to gut the inside, so she has a killer kitchen. The dream of a new kitchen was the only reason she finally conceded and let me buy something."

The fondness between mother and son was evident in Pete's voice as he talked about her. Kendall smiled. Ryan had bought their parents a new house when he'd started playing professionally. Unfortunately, her parents didn't have the same sentimental feelings as Pete's mom. Hers had been all too happy to take the upgrade and brag to anyone who'd listen about their professional athlete son. She'd grown up in Ryan's shadow and when he hit the Majors, it had become painfully clear she would never get out of his shadow. And frankly, she'd stopped trying.

"Did your mom give you any ideas about this place?" She was in awe of the design and thought that went into this apartment. Everywhere she looked there were carefully chosen elements. The pasta faucet on the wall behind the stove. The narrow drawers along the floor that held cookie sheets and pans. The wine cooler that at first glance looked like a piece of art designed to create some separation in the rooms. It was all beautiful and so well thought out.

"Sort of. When she was planning her kitchen, she felt the need to include me in every decision she made." He shook his head and laughed. "You should know what you are paying for," he said, imitating his mother's voice again.

The affection in his voice as he talked about his mom and her dreams made her stomach tighten. He was such a sweet guy. She'd never seen this side of him before this trip. Previously, Pete was always just her brother's dreamy friend. This gorgeous, fun guy her brother brought home occasionally. But this kind, sweet guy? Shoot, that was the kind of guy a woman could really fall for. She stood up and walked towards him. She needed to stop those kinds of thoughts right now. This was a week-long fling with a guy she'd had a crush on for years. Nothing more. She was not going to be stupid enough to start creating dreams about them.

She wrapped her arms around him as he stood at the stove. "It smells good."

Pete turned his head. "So do you," he replied, and pressed a kiss against her lips. "Now go sit down so I can feed you before you have to go to work."

She grabbed two mugs from the cupboard. "What do you take in your coffee?" she asked.

"Nothing, just black."

Kendall wrinkled her nose. Yuck. "Do you happen to have milk or cream?"

"There's milk. I can pick up some cream today when I'm out."

She filled the two cups and doctored her coffee with milk until it was a nice creamy color and sat down at the island. Pete slid a heaping plate of French toast in front of her, then placed syrup, icing sugar and some creamy concoction on the table.

She eyed the creamy substance. "What is that?"

"Maple syrup cream cheese. I just made it." He grabbed the bowl and scooped some of the cream cheese mixture onto his plate. "I didn't know what you liked on yours, so I just covered my bases."

"You really eat that on your French toast?"

"Yeah, of course. It's not French toast if you don't have lots of sugar. Everyone knows that."

"I'm just surprised you eat it. My brother is always watching what he puts in his mouth."

Pete smirked and raised an eyebrow. "Good to know."

"Ew, gross, that's not what I meant."

"I didn't say anything. You're the one with a sick mind. I just said it was good to know."

She flicked icing sugar at him with her fork, and he jumped back, laughing. "Hey, easy."

He brushed the icing sugar off his shirt. "I pay attention to what I eat, but life is too short not to enjoy things like icing sugar or cream cheese frosting on French toast. I exercise. I work hard. I deserve to enjoy it. Plus, it just tastes freaking good."

She picked up the maple cream cheese icing bowl and spread some on her French toast and took a big bite. "Oh my god, that is good."

"Right?" Pete put another bite in his mouth and nodded his head. "Worth a little extra time in the gym any day."

She finished her breakfast and loaded her dish into the dishwasher. Pete walked up behind her, grabbed her hips, and hoisted her up onto the counter. His warm hands pressed against her thighs to spread her legs, but her pencil skirt held them in place.

"Jesus, this thing is like a chastity belt," he said as he eased her skirt a bit higher on her thighs so he could step in between her legs.

He pressed his lips against hers. She sighed. God, this morning was like the pinnacle of all her youthful fantasies rolled into one. A sexy man cooking for her in the kitchen. That sexy man being freaking Pete Saunders was almost more than she could handle. She shuddered beneath his touch.

His tongue swiped against her bottom lip, and she parted her mouth, allowing him access. His tongue teased against hers, softly at first, then growing bolder, hungrier. Soon, they were both panting.

Pete rested his forehead against hers. "Shit, sorry, that was supposed to just be a light 'have a good day' kiss. I didn't mean for it to get so heavy." His fingers brushed her waistband. "Every time I touch you, I..." He broke off and exhaled. "I don't know what the fuck this is, Ken, but Jesus, you do something to me."

She licked her lips and smiled. "Believe me, the feeling is mutual."

His hard cock pulsed against her panties, and he shifted his hips against her body. She bit back a moan. Placing her hand on his chest, she pushed lightly. "I've gotta get to work and if I let you stay here like that..." She shifted her hips, pressing their bodies together. "I'll never get to the office."

Pete groaned and stepped back. "Fair enough. Are you free tonight?"

Kendall scanned his face. His green eyes were molten with lust and she chewed her bottom lip. She'd never wanted to ditch work to fuck someone ever before, but god did she want to skip out on work today and just curl up in bed with Pete.

"I should be off work at 5 and then I'll come straight back here."

He pressed a kiss to her lips. "Drive fast."

She giggled. "Will do."

CHAPTER FIVE

Forty-five minutes later, she strolled into the downtown office of Magnolia Designs. Kendall glanced around the reception area. The San Diego office was a delightful blend of southern charm and the western boho vibe of the community.

She walked up to the reception desk and smiled at the twenty-something blonde behind the desk. "Morning, I'm Kendall Graves. I'm here to see Mark Saul."

"Of course, follow me." She stood up from the desk. Kendall's eyes widened as she scanned the woman's outfit. There was clearly a difference between work attire at the two offices. There is no way Kendall would have gotten away with ripped jeans in the office in Atlanta. Although she had to give the woman props for her style. The baggy ripped jeans with high heels were super cute. Kendall glanced down at herself. Unfortunately, with her short frame, the outfit wouldn't look nearly the same on her as it did the supermodel statuesque receptionist.

She smoothed her hands down the front of her pencil skirt and followed the woman down the hallway. The woman rapped lightly on the open door. "Hey Mark, Kendall's here."

"Sorry, I didn't catch your name," Kendall said to the blonde.

"Simone."

"Nice to meet you." Kendall smiled at Simone before turning to face the man in the room. "Hey Mark, good to see you."

Mark pushed his trendy thick-rimmed glasses up on his nose, then stepped around to the front of his desk. "You too. Can I get you coffee or anything?"

"Sure, or maybe just point me in the right direction and I can grab it myself."

"Nah, it's fine. Simone will grab it for you. What do you take in it?" Mark asked.

"Cream please," she said, as she smiled at Simone.

"Grab me one too while you're at it, would you?" Mark asked.

Ouch. Kendall winced at the saccharine fake smile from Simone. Then she looked at Mark to see his reaction. Nothing. He appeared completely oblivious to the tension. *Interesting*.

She wandered to the window of Mark's office and looked down at the city street below. "I can't get over the differences between the two offices already, and I just got here."

"Yeah, we definitely prefer a more modern, hip vibe than the Atlanta office does."

Kendall bristled at the mocking tone and smirk on Mark's face. "I don't know that it's more hip, just different. Atlanta is established, well-known. It has roots and everyone knows what to expect." Kendall looked around

Mark's office, at the art on the walls and his hipster clothing. "I think the San Diego office is still new and trying to figure out its identity."

"We have an identity," Mark snapped.

"Okay." Kendall sat down in one of the two open chairs by Mark's desk. "What's the identity of this office? What type of new clients are you bringing in? I assume you're doing lots of new client meetings, so what is the new demographic?"

"I wouldn't say we have our target demographic nailed down yet. We are still fairly new."

Kendall leaned back in her chair and crossed her leg over her knee and pinned him with a stare. "Mark, come on, don't bullshit me. This is marketing 101. You're trying to tell me that the reason the numbers are low is that the Atlanta style doesn't fit in San Diego. What's your brand?"

"We're still working on that."

Good lord. Why did they hire this guy? Either he didn't have the first clue how to honestly run an office or he had a problem with a woman in authority and didn't want to discuss it with her. Either way, this was a problem.

Kendall took a deep breath and ran her tongue along the inside of her mouth to try to settle her stomach. Going off on this guy on day one was not the objective. She'd been told to come in, assess the situation and clean it up so they could get back on track.

She rubbed her palms together. "Okay Mark. Look, I understand that it's difficult to have someone new come into your house and want to change things. You wouldn't have been hired for this position if the board didn't feel you were the right person for the job. I know you must have great ideas, so walk me through them. I'm here to help. This is what I do and I'm damn good at my job, but you have to trust me if this is going to work."

"Right, I just think it's a little premature to have them send you in already. We are still getting our feet wet."

"Fair enough. It takes time to work out all the kinks and get things running smoothly. Believe me, I'm well aware of that. The problem is a few of our long-term clients are not happy with their service here."

Mark scoffed and puffed up in his chair. She held up her hand. "I'm not placing blame in the least. But if we are losing big contracts, there need to be new contracts to take their place. Who are you meeting with to replace the clients that are unhappy?"

"No one is going anywhere," Mark grumbled.

Was this guy for real? Kendall fought the urge to roll her eyes. They didn't pay her enough to pander to the ego of the thirty-five-year-old man-child in front of her. "Mark, First National is my client in Atlanta. That's why they are your client here and they're not happy with the service."

Mark shifted uncomfortably in his chair as Kendall watched him. "As you said, Mark, the West Coast is different from the East. What appeals to the bank's clients will be different to some degree, but at the end of the day, it's still a bank. People want stability, security, a sense of calm when it comes to their money. That doesn't change. I'm sure you had great ideas, but the client didn't feel like you heard them, and they didn't feel like you understood their product and unfortunately, in this industry, that's the kiss of death."

"I'm not an idiot, despite what you've been told."

"I know you aren't. So walk me through what your vision is for this office."

A light rapping on the door pulled Kendall's attention from her computer screen. She glanced up to find Simone standing in the doorway.

"Do you need anything before I head out for the night?" Simone asked.

Kendall glanced at the clock over her door. "Wow, I didn't realize it was 5 o'clock already. Thanks for the offer, but no, you can take off. I'll be leaving here in a minute as well. Thanks for all your help today, Simone."

"Were you able to make a dent in the files you were looking at?" Simone leaned her hip against the doorframe as she watched Kendall.

"Yeah, I think I have a pretty good handle on things now. Mark and the team have come up with some brilliant campaigns."

Simone wrinkled her nose, then quickly covered it with a smile. "Yeah, we have some good ones."

"What was that face for?" Kendall asked.

"What? Nothing." Simone pushed off from the wall. "Well, if you don't need anything else, I'll see you tomorrow."

"Absolutely. Have a great night." Kendall watched the other woman as she left her office. What had that face been about? Unfortunately, she had spent the majority of the day buried behind a computer screen, going over files and marketing plans. Tomorrow she would have to spend some time getting to know the team members better. In the few interactions she had witnessed today, it was clear Mark viewed himself as separate from the rest of the team. She just hadn't figured out what that meant for the office morale yet.

Kendall stretched her arms over her head and rolled her neck back and forth to ease her muscles after sitting all afternoon. She pushed away from the desk and pulled her purse out of the bottom desk drawer.

Holy shit, she was going home to Pete. Her stomach flipped as she imagined walking into his place and seeing him again. As a teenage girl, how many times had she daydreamed about being married to Pete Saunders and what their life would look like? And for this week, at least, she could pretend that it was real. She hooked her purse over her shoulder and quickly made her way to the elevator. She punched the elevator button and impatiently tapped her foot as she waited for the doors to slide open.

As the elevator doors opened, she felt someone walk up beside her. She glanced over her shoulder at the newcomer. "Karl, right?" she asked.

"Yep, that's me. How did your first day go?"

"It was good. Busy, but I was able to get a really good overview of the types of clients you've been working with recently. You did the work on that campaign for the surf shop, right?"

"Yeah, that was the most recent one I was working on."

"I loved it. You had some great ideas. From what I could see, it looks like you really connected with the client and understood the demographic."

"Yeah, well, I grew up here. Grew up surfing, so I am their demographic."

"Nothing wrong with that. Your understanding of the market was clear in the campaign."

"It's too bad it was such a small campaign, though," Karl replied.

"It wasn't that small. There's a decent potential for repeat business from them as well as some of the other stores in the area. If I remember correctly, there are several surfing competitions in the area, right?"

"Yeah, quite a few."

The doors to the elevator sprang open and together they walked towards their vehicles. Kendall glanced over at Karl. "So, there's lots of potential to tap into more of that market."

"Um, I guess, but Mark wants us to spend our time looking for bigger fish, so I haven't even looked at tapping into that."

"Big contracts are all well and good, but there's definitely a place for the smaller ones, especially in a boutique firm like ours."

"Tell Mark that," Karl muttered under his breath.

Kendall stopped at her rental. "Can we chat some more tomorrow? If you're free, we could maybe meet in the morning? I'd like to sit down individually with everyone before I dive into the team meetings, so I have a better idea of what everyone's strengths and goals are."

Karl chewed his lower lip as he looked at her. "Can I be really honest with you?"

"Of course."

"Why did Atlanta send you here? Are they looking at closing us down already?"

"Gosh no. I'm mostly here to get a better picture of who everyone on the team is so we can come up with some strategies for growth here in San Diego. Make sure that both offices are on the same page for what the support and services will look like. I have several national clients that need support on the west coast as well, so I'm just trying to get a feel for how we can make that work for them across the board. If it makes sense to divide things up between the offices or to keep everything in Atlanta, that kind of thing." She smiled at him and squeezed his arm. "Your job is definitely not in jeopardy because I'm here."

Karl exhaled audibly. "Good, Mark said you might chop some people if you didn't like what you saw."

What the hell? Why would Mark have told his staff that? That guy was a real piece of work. "No, you don't need to worry about that. And from what I saw today looking through your portfolio, you wouldn't need to worry, even if I was here for that purpose." She gave Karl what she hoped was a reassuring smile. "You can tell everyone they can relax. I'm not here to cut anyone's job. I'm here to help make this business as successful as possible and you all know the area better than I do. While I'm here, my door is open. If anyone has any ideas, please share them."

Karl pursed his mouth like he'd tasted something awful. "Yeah, I'm not sure Mark would be happy with us doing that."

"Well, that's a problem. In my experience, I've found working in this type of environment with other creative people it works best when ideas flow openly and freely. In the Atlanta office, even though one person is in charge of the account, we regularly meet with other people to bounce ideas and do whatever we can to get the creative juices flowing."

"I don't think that would work very well here."

"That's a shame, because it works really well for us in Atlanta. I don't want to keep you tonight since it's after hours, but if you could think about team dynamics. What your perfect team looks like and why for when we talk tomorrow that would be great. Like I said, I'm not here to change what's working well, but if something isn't working, that's helpful to know too and to see if we can make some tweaks."

"That sounds good and a lot less scary than what I was expecting." Karl pretended to wipe his brow. "Phew."

Kendall laughed. "Well, now you can go home and actually enjoy your evening rather than stressing about the awful lady from Atlanta who has come in to wreak havoc on the office."

"Definitely. You have a good night," Karl said as he turned toward his parked car.

Her mind raced as she climbed behind the wheel of the car. Why would Mark have scared all of his staff about their job security? The more she got to know this guy, the more confused she was about the decision to hire him. Hopefully tomorrow things would become clearer. She put the key in the ignition and fired up her rental.

As the car roared to life, a wave of excitement surged through her stomach. A smile split across her face at the prospect of spending the evening with Pete. She threw the car into reverse and hit the gas. The tires squealed against the shiny parkade pavement in her haste to get home. She winced at the screeching noise and eased her foot off the gas. "Real cool, Ken, real cool," she muttered to herself.

She rolled down the window, pointed the car in the direction of Pete's place and wove into rush hour traffic. Just because she was excited to see Pete didn't mean she had to be quite so obvious. One thing she'd learned growing up around her brother was it was never a good thing when a woman made it too easy. Competitive guys were competitive everywhere. And she intended to win this little game she and Pete were playing.

CHAPTER SIX

At the sound of the front door opening, Pete glanced up from his stool at the kitchen island.

"Hey, I'm back," Kendall said as she closed the door behind her.

He allowed his eyes to linger on her as she walked towards him. Captivated by the movement of her hips in the tight pencil skirt, he licked his lips. Damn. Did she always look this good, and he was just too stupid to notice it? He'd always known she was pretty but the Kendall he remembered and this Kendall were night and day different when it came to outright pure sex appeal. He couldn't look at her and not want to take her against the closest available surface.

She stopped in front of him and cocked her hip against the island. When he glanced at her face, she smiled and raised her eyebrow coyly at him.

All right, not his smoothest showing. He cleared his throat. "How was your day?"

"Overall, I think it was good. Little bumpy in a few places, but on the whole I think it went well. How was yours?"

"Yeah, good, pretty laid back. Went for a run, then met Gonzo and Smitty for a workout. Getting all geared up for next week."

"Are you leaving on Saturday or Sunday?"

"Sunday. Camp starts on Monday, but they don't need any of us there until Tuesday. The coaches want to get a look at all the newbies first and they have lots of meetings and discussions for them on day one."

"That's nice that you get out of that. Does Ryan too, or does he have to sit through it all because he's already there?"

"Well, he'll be training already, so they'll probably pull him into some of the afternoon stuff."

"Right, that makes sense." She pulled out the stool beside him. His eyes stayed riveted to her as she shifted her skirt above her knee and crossed her legs. The muscles in her legs flexed with the movement and he wanted to run his hand up her calf.

With a herculean effort, he pulled his gaze back to her face. "You want a drink or anything?" he asked.

"No, I'm good."

"You up for doing something active tonight, or are you too tired after your day?"

Kendall's eyes darkened and a sexy smile curled up the corner of her full lips. "What did you have in mind?"

Jesus. "Did you bring a bathing suit?"

Her eyes narrowed and she smirked as she watched him warily. "Yes, why?"

"I was thinking it would be fun to take the standup paddleboards out for a spin."

Kendall's face brightened. The sexy smile that had been there a moment before was replaced by a wide-eyed excitement he hadn't seen on anyone's face in longer than he could remember. Nostalgic memories filled his brain. This was the Kendall he remembered. The girl who was always up for any adventure. Nothing was too dangerous or crazy for her to want to try. She'd been full of energy, annoying at times in her effort to always be with the guys. She'd idolized her brother. Always tagging along, but barely saying two words to Pete. He could still picture all the times Ryan had warned off some little shit that was sniffing around his sister. A wave of guilt crashed into his chest. Fuck, now he was the little shit sniffing around her.

"Can we do that from here?" Kendall asked.

"Yeah, we can just put in from the dock out back."

"I am so jealous that you have that option right out in your backyard."

Needing to put some space between them, he pushed away from the counter. "All right, let's do it. I'll meet you back here in five."

"Are we going to be warm enough?"

"Yeah, we'll be fine. The water is still pretty cold, so I have a wetsuit for you down on the dock."

"Okay, give me five and I'll meet you out back."

After quickly slipping into his boardshorts, he wandered outside. He sat on the back step as he waited for Kendall and tilted his face up to the sky, letting the warmth of the sun beat down on his skin. Man, he loved California. When he'd been drafted to San Diego two years ago, he'd thought he'd died and gone to heaven. Growing up in Vegas, he was used to the heat, but having access to the ocean was like a dream he hadn't even known he wanted. There was just something about the ocean that spoke to him in a way he couldn't describe.

The door behind him snicked open and he shifted around. "Fuck," he muttered when he saw Kendall standing above him in a skimpy green bikini.

"What?" Kendall asked, her eyes wide as she looked down at him.

Pushing to his feet, he sucked in a deep breath before turning back around to face her. He allowed his gaze to scan down her body, then slowly back up. Living here, he saw women in bathing suits regularly. But Kendall in a bikini? Damn.

"Wow," he said and wrapped his arm around her waist, pulling her tightly against him. "Maybe I changed my mind and we should just stay here."

"Not a chance, buddy. You promised me paddle-boarding and we are paddle-boarding." She pushed against his chest.

"Yeah, but that was before I saw what you looked like in a bikini."

Kendall snorted. "You saw me naked last night. What my body looks like in a bathing suit can't be that much of a surprise."

"Last night I was drunk with lust. My eyes weren't fully focused because all the blood had left my head." He stepped back so he could look at her again. "Now my eyes are working properly and..." He shook his head. "It's a good thing it's cold enough for us to need wetsuits, otherwise I don't think I'd be able to stand up on my board."

"Shut up." She smacked his arm. "Do you have keys for this?" She nodded towards the door.

"Don't need it. There's just a code."

"Oh, that's handy."

"Yeah, it makes it a lot easier to go for a run or a swim when I don't have to worry about carrying keys and crap."

He handed her a towel and they strolled down to the dock.

"Is Ryan's place on the water? I haven't seen it yet."

"No, he's up on a hill overlooking the valley. I think you can probably see the water from some places on the property, but I'm not entirely sure."

"I can't believe he wouldn't live near the ocean. That's crazy."

Pete didn't understand why you wouldn't live on the water if you could afford it either, but then Ryan was looking for different things in a home than Pete was. "His place looks pretty amazing. It's got a great pool and outdoor living space so he can have everyone over."

"I guess, but a pool isn't the ocean."

"You got me there. But then I bought an old warehouse so I could live on the water, so I'm not sure I'm the best one to talk to about Ry's house choice."

Once on the dock, Pete handed her a wetsuit. "Hopefully, I got the size right."

Kendall smiled at him shyly. "You bought me a wetsuit."

He scrubbed the back of his neck. Why was she looking at him like that? It was a wetsuit, not a pony. "I figured if I wanted you to go in the water with me, you'd need to be warm."

Kendall stood up on tiptoes and pressed a kiss to his lips. "Thank you, that's very sweet."

"Sure," he mumbled. He stepped into his suit and shifted until he could pull the material over his hips. Turning, he caught a glimpse of Kendall and his mouth went dry as he watched her shimmy herself into the neoprene fabric. He'd thought covering her up would be better, but the thing fit like a second skin, emphasizing her curves and the roundness of her hips.

"Right." He cleared his throat. "Have you ever paddle-boarded before?"

"No, but I've done lots of windsurfing, so hopefully that transfers." She secured her lifejacket around herself and he breathed a sigh of relief. Thank god, the bulky jacket covered most of her body. He couldn't imagine anything worse than sporting a hard-on in a skintight wetsuit. It was bad enough in jeans, let alone in this monstrosity.

"You're athletic. You should be fine." He handed her a paddle and explained how to measure it for herself and waited for her to adjust it.

He dropped her board into the water off the side of the dock and held it in place. "Hop on. Start on your knees and then you can push yourself to standing once you get away from the dock."

Kendall smirked at him. "Afraid I'll fall and crack my skull, are you?"

"The thought crossed my mind." He laughed. "Nah, it's just easier to stand once you have a feel for the board underneath yourself, and you can't really do that if you're holding onto the dock."

Kendall hopped onto the board and pushed away from the dock while resting on her knees. After securing his dry bag to the front, Pete set his board in and followed suit. "I thought we'd just paddle near the shoreline for today to give you a chance to get used to things."

"Sounds good."

He stood up and paddled beside her board. After several strokes, Kendall still hadn't stood up. "You just going to stay on your knees?"

"I'm scared I might fall in and the water is freaking cold."

"You aren't going to fall. There're barely any waves. You'll be fine."

"All right," she said skeptically, as she braced herself on her hands and pushed to a stand. She wobbled a bit before gaining her balance. "Ok, I think I've got it."

They paddled side by side for several minutes without speaking. This was one of his favorite ways to spend the afternoon. Normally he went out by himself, but it was kind of nice having Kendall along.

"So, you said you worked out with some teammates today?" Her voice broke through the silence.

"Yeah, Gonzo and Smitty."

"Gonzo and Smitty. I haven't quite figured out all your teammates yet and don't know their nicknames."

"Gonzo is Ramon Gonzalez. He plays third."

"Ok, yep, I know who he is. The nickname makes sense."

Pete laughed. Ballplayers loved to give each other nicknames, and often what they came up with made no sense. Hell, he'd been nicknamed Zip ever since an announcer had said he zipped around the field at the Little League World Series and the name just kind of stuck.

"And who is Smitty?" Kendall asked.

"Centerfielder, Jeff Smith."

"Jeff Smith, I can't picture what he looks like."

"I don't know. He looks like a regular dude with brownish-blond hair."

"A regular dude?" Kendall laughed. "Real descriptive. I know exactly what he looks like now."

"Shut up." He laughed. "I don't know. He looks like a regular guy who plays centerfield. Kind of lean, average height, his hair is a bit lighter than mine. He looks like a ballplayer."

Kendall dropped the paddle into the water and flicked it at him, spraying him. "Hey." He shifted on his board to try to get away from the cool water. "Watch it." He dipped his paddle in the water and aimed it towards her like he was going to shoot her back.

"Don't you dare. I'll fall in for sure," Kendall said nervously. She dug her paddle into the water and tried to paddle out of his reach.

"Don't start something if you aren't willing to deal with the consequences," he teased.

"Truce. I'm sorry." She giggled.

The sound of a boat roaring up the coast caught his attention. "Shit," he muttered. "You may want to kneel down. The waves can be kind of brutal when boats get too close."

"It should be fine. There's no reason for him to get close," Kendall replied.

A few seconds later, the boat roared past them, significantly closer than he needed to. Their laughter was audible over the booming music on board. The waves crashed against the side of the board and it took all of his skill not to pitch into the water. The splash to his right said Kendall wasn't so lucky. Her board launched past him on a wave.

She popped back up out of the water and squealed. "Holy shit, it's cold."

He paddled over to her and hoisted her up on his board since hers was currently heading towards the shoreline. "Now, do you see why I said you should wear the ankle strap?" he asked.

"Nope, I still say I would have drowned if that thing was tied to me." She shivered and her whole body shook. He kneeled down and wrapped his arms around her, effectively pulling her onto his lap. Okay, maybe there were some perks to her not being attached to her board. Kendall curled up against him. Her breath was hot against his neck and she snuggled closer, trying to get his warmth.

"We should go get the board," she said, her teeth chattering noisily as she spoke.

"It's fine. It's not going anywhere." He sat down and pulled her back against his chest, securing her tightly between his legs so he could wrap his body around her. "Sorry, I didn't think you'd be this cold if you fell in. I swim practically every day, so I didn't realize how cold it would be to someone who isn't used to it."

"It's probably not that cold. I'm like this in the summer too. As much as I love the water, I do see the appeal to a heated pool." She pressed back against him. "Besides, this is kind of nice."

Finally, her shivering stopped and she sighed. "I guess we should go grab my board before it's destroyed from hitting the breakwater."

"Probably," he grumbled, surprised by how much he wanted to say fuck it and just stay as they were. He wasn't normally a cuddly guy. In his mind, cuddling served one purpose, to get laid. Once that was said and done, he normally dipped out. So, what the hell was different about Kendall? He rolled his eyes at himself. God, he was being such a girl. He felt bad that she was cold. That's all this was, nothing more.

He pushed himself up so he was standing. She shifted her body and glanced up at him. His dick twitched to life, seeing her sitting there looking up at him. Her gaze flicked to his crotch and she licked her lips. She may as well have licked his cock since the simple look sent all the blood to that part of his body. The way she affected him was unreal. He hadn't been this quick on the draw since he was a teen. Needing to get things back on a more even keel, he looked down at her and waggled his eyebrows. "While you're down there," he joked.

Kendall smacked him on the leg. "Yeah, that's never going to happen."

"Never?"

She glanced around. "Not out here, no."

Damn it, that made his dick twitch even more. "Meaning it's not out of the question if we were someplace else?"

Her eyes darkened as she looked up at him. "It's not out of the question."

"Hang on," he said as he dug his paddle into the water and surged the board forward.

Kendall giggled. "I didn't say we'd do that now."

"That's not what I heard," he called as he eagerly paddled towards her board. As far as he was concerned, they couldn't get home fast enough. Whether or not a blowjob was on the table, Kendall was definitely on the menu, and he was starving.

Thursday afternoon, Kendall glanced at the clock on the wall. Two-thirty. Only half an hour more and Pete would be coming to pick her up so she could slip out of work early. She clicked on the email that had just arrived in her inbox and sighed in exasperation.

Seriously? This was the kind of email Mark sent out to an employee? She forwarded the email to the Atlanta office. Standing up, she walked over to the door and clicked it shut. The last thing she needed was Mark popping his head in when she was talking to their bosses about him.

She put her earbuds in and dialed her boss Sandra's number. After three rings, Sandra picked up.

"Hi Kendall, what's up?" Sandra's warm voice glided over the line.

"I just forwarded you an email. Do you want to take a look at it and get back to me tomorrow, since I'm sure you're getting ready to head home soon?"

"No, hang on and I'll look at it while I have you on the phone," Sandra replied. Kendall could hear her moving around the office.

"Did I catch you at a bad time?"

"No, I was just on my way out, but I'll look at this now so I can put it out of my mind for the rest of the evening."

"I'm not sure if that's true," Kendall muttered.

"Are you fucking kidding me?" Sandra yelled.

Kendall winced and turned down the volume on her phone.

"Please tell me he is not that big of an idiot," Sandra asked.

Kendall glanced at the email on her screen again and winced when she saw the lewd comment he had made to Simone. "Apparently he is."

"Remind me who Simone is exactly."

"She's the receptionist at the front desk," Kendall replied.

"How does she come across?"

"What do you mean? Like how does she look? Or do I think she'll be cool and not try to sue the company for sexual harassment?"

"Son of a—" Sandra blurted. "Do we need to worry about a lawsuit?"

"I don't think so. When she came in earlier today to talk to me about the email, she seemed like she just wanted me to talk to him, so he'd back off. I asked her to forward the email to me so I could speak to him about it."

"One, how can he be that stupid to put something in writing, and two, how were we so blind that we didn't see what kind of asshole we'd hired?"

"The problem is, he didn't actually say anything."

"What are you talking about? Of course he said something. It's pretty clear he's trying to get in Simone's pants," Sandra roared.

"I know, but when you read it again, you'll see what I'm talking about. He's crafty. Smart enough to use innuendo without outright saying anything, so I don't know if you can legally say he sexually harassed her," Kendall glanced at the email again. It was cringy, but a guy like Mark could easily say it was misinterpreted and he was just watching out for Simone as the boss, not being pervy by pointing things out. Gross.

"Maybe," Sandra grumbled.

"What do you want me to do? It's not really my place to talk to him about this since that's more something you four would need to do."

Kendall could hear the click click of Sandra tapping her pen on her desktop, a sure sign she was deep in thought. The tapping grew more rapid and Kendall grimaced. "Sorry to ruin your evening with all this."

"No, it's fine, not your fault." Tap, tap, tap. "You must be doing a good job there if Simone felt comfortable enough to come talk to you about this."

"Thanks," Kendall replied. "Yeah, I think I'm building a pretty good rapport with most of the team. There's a lot of talent here. The problem is Mark doesn't let them use it. He feels the need to flex his muscles on every account and it seems to stifle productivity in a big way."

"And now we have this to worry about as well." Kendall heard Sandra's chair wheels glide across the floor. "I'll have to speak to everyone tonight and get back to you later when we have a plan. I'm going to have to speak to our lawyer because we can't just up and fire him without making sure we are legally protected." Sandra sighed. "What a cluster."

"I knew he had an ego, but I just didn't imagine—" She paused as she tried to figure out how to explain it to Sandra. "I mean, Simone is hungry and made no bones about the fact that she wants to advance here. I just can't believe Mark would use that against her to try to get laid. What a creep."

"Is Simone someone that you would promote?"

"Too soon to tell. I don't know her well enough to know what she'd be like in any other role. She's competent where she is, I can say that, but anything else? No idea. When we talked, I suggested she take some distance classes to gain some more skills and training, because from an educational standpoint she's underqualified."

"Okay, that's helpful for me to know when I speak to the lawyer. We aren't going to promote her just because of Mark."

"I don't think that's what she was looking for," Kendall replied. When she'd spoken to Simone, she'd been embarrassed and thought she'd given Mark the wrong idea about her. Kendall had done her best to smooth things over and felt like the conversation went well. She'd pull her aside again tomorrow and see how she was doing.

"I hate to ask you this, Kendall, but is there any way you could stay another week to give us some time to get things sorted out?"

"Umm... I don't know. The person I'm staying with is leaving for a month on Sunday, so..."

"We can put you up in a hotel if need be. Of course, we were happy to save the expense this week when you said you had someplace to stay, but we were prepared to pay for it when we first agreed to send you there."

"OK, let me talk to Pete and see if I can stay next week, and I'll let you know when we talk tomorrow."

Kendall could hear Sandra's frustration when she exhaled loudly over the phone. "I'll get back to you tomorrow after I've spoken to the lawyer."

"Sounds good. Have a good night," Kendall said.

"You too. Are you still going to be able to leave early today?"

"Yeah, I think so. If he hasn't left already, Mark should be leaving soon, and then he'll be out of the office the rest of the afternoon in meetings, but Brad is here so any problems can be brought to him."

"Good. I keep forgetting about the time change when I start texting you in the morning, so you deserve some time off to make up for it. I can't tell you how much we all appreciate you being willing to take all this on for us, Kendall. There's no one we trust more to be there when one of us can't."

"Oh, thank you. I really appreciate you saying that." She glanced up at the clock. Pete would be there in five minutes. "Try not to work all night," she told her boss.

"I won't. Not much we can do till we speak to the lawyer about the best way to get rid of the weasel we stupidly hired. I have a feeling he's going to say this isn't enough to outright fire him and we'll have to send him to sensitivity training or something ridiculous first."

Why was it so hard to fire a lousy employee? Kendall hung up the phone. She chewed on her bottom lip and looked around the office. Should she cancel on Pete and stay at work? There wasn't much she could do about things today. Besides, her bosses were the ones who needed to figure things out. Her hands were pretty much tied despite the fact she wanted to grab Mark by the balls and twist. There was nothing worse than someone using their power like that.

A knock sounded at her office door. "Come in," she called.

Simone pushed open the door. "You have a visitor," she said, waggling her eyebrows. "Do you want me to send him back?"

"Yes, please." Kendall's stomach flipped. How did he still have this effect on her? If anything, her reaction to him had intensified over the past few days.

Kendall grabbed the files from her desk and walked over to the filing cabinet to put them away for the night. She turned at the light rapping on the door. Pete leaned negligently against the frame, one foot crossed over the other. "So, this is where the magic happens?"

"Something like that. I'm not sure how magically I'm doing anything, but this is where I'm working. Come on in. I just need to shut down my computer and I'll be ready."

He pushed away from the door and wandered into the room. The office seemed to shrink in half at his presence. "No rush, we've got time and I'm a couple of minutes early."

Pete dropped down onto the chair and watched her intently.

"Stop staring," she mumbled.

"Why? I like looking at you and I've never seen you in your natural environment before."

Kendall scrunched up her nose and mock scowled at him. "This isn't the zoo."

A loud crash sounded down the hall, followed by a squeal and laughter. "Are you sure?" he asked.

"Okay, so maybe it can be." She quickly hit the refresh button on her email. Nothing new, thank god. While the computer powered off, she quickly tidied the top of her desk. She could feel Pete watching her every movement. Raising her head, she glanced at him. "What? Why are you smirking?"

"I'm not. I should've known you wouldn't be able to leave your office a mess."

"I can't help it. I just don't like to arrive in the morning and feel like I need to clean before I start the day."

"Fair enough." He picked up a pen from the edge of the desk and dropped it in the holder. "You are the cleanest house guest I've ever seen, so I wouldn't expect anything else in your office."

"I can be dirty," she grumbled.

A sexy half smile curved across his face. "Oh, believe me, I'm well aware."

Her cheeks heated at the innuendo, and she shifted her weight beneath his stare. Pete stood and walked around to her side of the desk. "I like it. All buttoned up and proper, but dirty when it matters."

She pressed her hand against his chest to hold him at bay. "Uh-uh, mister. Not happening here. My office is definitely one of those clean and proper places."

Pete eyed the desk, then raised his brow as he looked at her. "That's a shame." He stepped back, putting space between them. "But I can respect that. It's not like you could show up at my workplace and get lucky either."

"Could you imagine? Just drag you into the dugout." She giggled. That would go over well. Strolling onto the ball field in the middle of practice and pulling him off to have her way with him. Her gaze landed on Pete. Heat flared between them.

"Damn, now I really wish you would show up at my work," he said. His gaze trailed down her body as he pulled his bottom lip between his teeth.

She felt the look all the way to her core. Damn, the man was potent.

Shaking off the lustful fog, Kendall took a deep breath. "All right, let's get out of here before I let you coerce me into making a career-ending mistake on this desk."

"Nah, as hot as that would be, I'd never do anything that would put your job in jeopardy. Even I'm not that big of a jerk."

"You're not a jerk at all."

Pete scoffed. "Trust me, I definitely can be."

"Well, can't we all?" Kendall asked. She grabbed her purse out of her bottom drawer and slung it over her shoulder. "I'm ready."

"After you," Pete said as he stepped back to allow her to precede him out of the office. She stopped at the reception desk. "Simone, I'm gone for the day."

"Okay, have fun," she said.

"Oh, and I'm working on what we talked about earlier and hope to know a bit more tomorrow." Kendall made eye contact with Simone and held her stare, hoping to instill some confidence that she was on top of this, and it would not be brushed under the rug.

"Thanks, I appreciate it. Now get out of here and enjoy the rest of your afternoon."

Kendall rapped the top of the desk with her knuckles. "See you tomorrow."

Pete followed her to the elevator, and neither of them spoke while they waited for the doors to open. Once inside, Pete leaned against the railing and looked at her. "Everything okay?"

"What?"

"You sure you can leave the office early?"

"Of course I can. Why do you ask?"

He shrugged. "I don't know. It just seemed like you were relaying some kind of important message back there."

She cocked her head to the side as she looked at him. Who knew Pete Saunders was so observant? Most people watching that interaction wouldn't have given it a second thought, and here Pete was willing to put his plans on hold so she could take care of a work issue. She stepped toward him and his eyes widened. She leaned in and pressed a kiss against his lips. "Thank you. I appreciate the concern. It's very sweet. But I'm all yours this afternoon. I'm dying to see this project you want to show me."

Pete pushed his sandy brown hair away from his forehead and rubbed the back of his neck nervously.

"What?" she asked.

"I don't know. Now that I've asked you to come, I'm kind of worried you'll think I'm stupid for wanting to try this. It's a little out of my wheelhouse."

They strolled side by side through the parking garage towards his SUV. "Why would I think you're stupid? Not that I can answer that since you've been kind of evasive about everything."

Inside the car, he fired it to life and backed out of the stall. "I haven't been evasive, I've just...I don't know...I don't usually share this side of my life with anyone, so it's a bit weird."

"Well, I'm honored you asked me to come." She shifted in her seat and faced him as he wove the car through traffic. "Where are we going?"

"We're going to look at apartment complexes."

"What? Why would we be doing that? I thought you said we were meeting with a charity you're involved with."

"Yeah, we are. It's called Trust, Hope and Helping Hands. They work predominantly with single moms. They've been around for several years and have been doing some great work." He glanced over at her. "I've been talking with the executive director, Janelle, a lot about the barriers and affordable housing is always the biggest one."

"That makes sense. Rent is so expensive, especially in the city."

"Exactly, and moving isn't an option when you need to be close to work. Some of the issues can be handled fairly easily with organizations like this, clothing for job interviews, after-school programs, free school supplies, that kind of thing. It can be a real balancing act to juggle all the balls necessary to keep a family afloat."

Kendall watched Pete as he spoke passionately about the organization. "But housing is a whole other ballgame?" Kendall asked.

"Absolutely. Unfortunately, most of the lower income houses are kind of gross. It's one thing to move in there as a single guy, but to bring your children into that environment is something else entirely."

"You sound like you are speaking from experience?" Kendall gently pressed.

"Yeah, I am. We lived in some real shitholes when my dad left. It was tough." He paused, the lines on his forehead furrowed and his jaw clenched. He exhaled roughly and rubbed his hand across his mouth before he appeared to shake off the painful memories. "I watched my mom scrape to put food on the table, working two jobs and my sports?" He shook his head and sighed. "I'm all too familiar with organizations like this one."

"I didn't know that." The Pete she remembered was cocky and so self-assured she never dreamed he'd grown up living hand to mouth. "But I thought you went to a pretty nice school in Vegas."

"Yeah, I did for middle school." He laughed, but the sound didn't hold much humor. "My mom signed me up for ball when I was little, mostly to give me something to do, but she chose baseball because there was a program that funded free ball for all kids. And the rest is history."

"Um, I think you left out something there in the retelling. How did you end up at a nice middle school? Did your mom get a different job?"

"Yeah, sort of. Turns out I was pretty good at ball and this little league team wanted me, but we didn't live in the district." He laughed again, but this time it was an honest laugh. "My mom may not have had money, but she wasn't dumb. She's a shrewd negotiator. She was able to wrangle herself a job as the school cook in exchange for me being able to attend. One of the families had a guest house on their property that we were able to stay in for the first year until we got on our feet. That's how I met my buddy Jax.

"He went to that school?"

"He sure did. It was his place we lived at. His dad was a dick, but Jax was cool, or he was, once we worked out our differences." He chuckled absently, as if he was remembering exactly what they'd worked out. "Things for my mom and I really turned around when we moved there. She was a lot happier after that and I busted my ass to make sure no one regretted letting us in."

"Wow. I had no idea."

"Yeah, my mom worked really hard for me to chase this dream, she sacrificed alot and we got lucky. Not everyone does."

"So now you want to help other families."

"Yeah. It seems like it's the least I can do, you know. I mean, if it wasn't for being able to play free ball, who knows where I would have ended up?"

"So affordable housing? How are you helping with that?"

"I'm thinking of buying a building and having the organization run it as low-income housing for families."

"Seriously?" In her excitement, Kendall clasped Pete's arm. "Oh my god, Pete, that's amazing."

He dropped his head and a blush ran up his neck. The fact he was embarrassed about what he wanted to do was even more endearing. Could he be any sweeter?

"So, how would it work?" she pressed.

Pete glanced over at her and a huge smile split across his face. "You don't think I'm an idiot for wanting to do this?"

"Are you kidding me? No, I think this is amazing. And really freaking hot."

"Yeah?" He grinned. "Well, maybe you can show me how hot when we get back to my place later."

"Oh, you can count on it." She leaned across the console and kissed the side of his face. "I'm very impressed."

"Well, it's not a done deal yet, so don't be too impressed."

"Pete, the fact that you are even exploring this as an option is fantastic. Very few people care enough to even think about doing something like this."

"That's kind of the problem. There's a lot of logistics involved in how to make this work as a charitable venture. I've been meeting a lot with the accountants and—" He sighed. "It's a bit of a pain, but I'm hoping it will all be worth it."

"Okay, so today how many complexes are we looking at?"

"Three." Pete reached over and squeezed her hand. "Thanks for this. I thought it'd be up your alley and I'm glad I was right."

"Honestly, my brain is spinning. What have you been using to market to your investors?"

"Um, I wouldn't say market and I haven't really figured out the whole investor thing too much. I've mentioned it to a couple people and just told them what I'm doing and said more money would help and they should give some because it's a good cause."

"Oh, my god." She shook her head. "Well, you're lucky you have a marketing guru in your vehicle because I could create the sweetest marketing campaign for fundraisers for this."

"Seriously, you'd want to help with this?"

"Are you kidding me? Of course I would."

"Thanks, Ken. That means the world to me. But we aren't there yet. Today we are just looking at places to see what's out there, and then we need to play with the numbers to see if it'll all work."

"No, I get it. Just know that the offer is there and I'm happy to do it on my own time for free."

"You don't have to do that."

"I want to. This is important to you and I want to help."

The GPS announced they would arrive at their destination in five hundred meters. Pete scowled, drawing Kendall's attention off him and back to their surroundings. The neighborhood looked a little rough but overall, not bad.

"Maybe it's better inside," she said.

"Probably isn't much worse." He pulled the car to a stop beside a silver sedan and a small middle-aged woman waved, then exited the car.

"That's Janelle," Pete told her. He flashed her a tight smile. "All right, let's go have a look."

CHAPTER SEVEN

Kendall sat on the edge of the bed and watched as Pete packed up his bags for the month.

"Are you sure it's okay that I stay here another week?" she asked.

"Of course, why wouldn't it be?" Pete stepped out of the closest with a pile of sportswear in his hand and started shoving it into his suitcase.

With a wince, she pushed him out of the way and dumped out his clothes on the bed.

"Hey what are you doing? I just packed that," he complained.

"I know, but the way you have this packed, your clothes will look like fish guts when you get there."

"Who cares? It's just training camp. I'll be wearing my uniform most of the time, and those things are indestructible."

She eyed his stack of button up shirts that he had folded right down the middle of the back and sighed.

"Do you know how hard it is to get that crease out if you fold it like this?"

He shrugged. "The hotel has a person you can hire to do your ironing for you. I just usually give them all my stuff when I get there and then it magically appears in my closet, ironed and looking all good."

"Oh, my god. You are so spoiled." She picked up the shirt and shook it out so she could fold it properly for packing. "Just because you can pay someone to do the work for you doesn't mean you can't make their job a little bit easier, princess."

Pete slapped his hand over his heart. "Princess? Ouch. That hurts. I'll have you know I tip them very well for their hard work because I totally appreciate the fact that they can do that for me since I freaking hate ironing. It's like something from Dante's circles of hell."

Kendall smirked. "Oh yeah, you think if you land in hell it'll just be you holding an iron, fighting to get creases out for the rest of your life?"

"You laugh, but it could happen. I mean, the steam and the heat?" He shrugged. "I'm just saying."

He plopped down on the bed and watched her fold his shirt. "I kind of like having you pack for me. Feels all domestic and shit."

He waggled his eyebrows at her, and she scowled back at him. "Grab a shirt and learn how to fold properly," she said as she tossed a plaid shirt at him.

"Fine."

"So, back to what I asked. You sure you're cool with me being here when you aren't?"

Pete stopped folding and looked over at her, his face wrinkled with confusion. "Why wouldn't I be?"

"I don't know. I just don't want you to think I'm going to get the wrong idea or anything."

"Like what? You planning on robbing me while I'm away?"

Kendall smacked him on the arm. "No, of course not. I just don't want you to think that I think this is more than what it is."

"Relax, Ken. I don't think I'm going to come home and find you've moved in or left pictures of yourself in every room, so I won't forget you," he mocked. He nudged her with his hip and she stopped what she was doing to look at him. Dressed in his low-slung sweats and fitted t-shirt, he looked like exactly what he was, a professional athlete.

The tail end of his shoulder tattoo peaked out the bottom of his sleeve. She licked her lips. Memories of tracing her tongue along the body of the Viking wolf tattoo made her breasts pull tight. God, that night had been incredible.

Pete's voice broke through her lust filled thoughts. "This week has been amazing. Better than I could have imagined, but like we talked about. This is a one off. A fun week, like vacation. Once you head back to Atlanta, it's done," Pete said.

"You still want that?" she asked. She held her breath while she waited, secretly hoping he might have changed his mind.

"Of course. Why wouldn't I?"

"No, you wouldn't," she said. She picked up another shirt off the bed. God, she hoped her voice sounded like she was cool about things going back to normal. The idea of Pete knowing how badly she wanted to continue this when he clearly didn't was mortifying.

He grabbed her shoulder and turned her so she was facing him. "You okay?"

"Yeah, of course. Why wouldn't I be?" she asked. *Oh god, please let my poker face be intact.*

"You just seemed funny there for a second. You're still cool with us just going back to normal, right? I mean, we talked about all this a lot."

"Of course I am. It would be stupid to try to continue something with you here and me there and everything with Ryan. It wouldn't make sense."

"Good, I'm glad we're both still on the same page." He wrapped his arms around her waist and pulled her up against him. "That doesn't mean I didn't really fucking enjoy this week with you." He nipped the cord of her neck and goosebumps broke out across her skin. "I wish I didn't have to go to Arizona this afternoon."

"Mmm, me too," she groaned as she tilted her head to the side to give him better access to her neck.

"Fuck, why do I still want you so much?" he groaned. "This is crazy." He placed his hands on her hips and picked her up, encouraging her to wrap her legs around his waist. "It's a good thing you don't live here or I'd have trouble keeping my hands off you around your brother and that would be a disaster."

"Good thing." But was it? Unfortunately, it didn't feel like a good thing. She'd been hoping that this week together would get Pete out of her system once and for all. As he lay her on the mattress and followed her down, she shivered beneath his touch. She feared it had done the opposite and she was more in love with him than ever. What a mess.

He was right, cutting things off cold turkey was for the best. That didn't mean she couldn't make the most of what time she had left.

She threaded her fingers in his hair and pulled his lips down to hers. Their tongues collided in a hungry, desperate kiss. She pushed his sweats down his hips, needing to feel him against her one last time.

He broke the kiss, sat up, and reached into the bedside table for a condom. He held the condom in his hand and stared down at her, breathing hard.

"What?" she asked when he didn't move.

"I'm just really torn on how I want this last time to be." He licked his lips. "Part of me wants to just fucking feast on every inch of you till I'm so full I never forget what you taste like."

She fought to breathe as she shivered beneath his stare. "That sounds good," she sighed. "What's the other thing you want to do?"

"Fuck you like this, when you're practically fully dressed, because I'm desperate to have you and can't wait. It feels kind of poetic because it's wrong and just fucking dirty and raw and—," he gritted the words out through clenched teeth. The look in his eyes was so hot she felt it all the way to her core. She wanted to clamp her legs together to ease the tension, but with the way he was sitting, his body held her open.

"Wow, umm, do we have time for both?" she asked.

"I'll make time. But the hotel is going to have to do some ironing."

Kendall giggled. "It'll be money well spent."

Pete walked up to the plate and stared down the pitching machine. The bastard wouldn't get the best of him today.

He rolled his shoulders and lined up. The first pitch soared over the plate, swing and a miss. *Fuck.* Pete nodded at the hitting coach to let him know he was ready, and the ball soared towards him again. Foul ball. Son of a bitch, what the hell was wrong with him?

Normally, when he stepped up to the plate, he felt a sense of calm go through his body. Hitting had always been his favorite part of the game. Some guys dreaded it, but for Pete, it was the reason he loved playing baseball.

As a kid, the crack of the bat against the ball had released stress he didn't even know he'd been holding. At first, it was a way to take out his anger and aggression. How many times had he pictured his dad's face as he hit the ball? But over the years, it had become therapeutic. It wasn't just the release of getting rid of energy and hitting something, but the skill involved in lining up his hit, aiming the ball, besting his opponent.

When he was at the plate, this was his house. It didn't matter what stadium he was in, he owned it in that moment. So what the fuck was wrong with his sticks? Because he sure as shit wasn't in the zone right now.

He continued to swing and hit the ball, but it didn't feel as smooth as it normally did. Joe Piper, the hitting coach, strolled over to him and Pete winced.

"You doing okay, Petey?"

"Yeah, I'm all good."

Joe's eyes narrowed as he looked at him. "You sure? You seem a little off."

"No, I'm all good. I was getting into the swing of things there at the end. Just a little rusty, I guess."

"Don't get me wrong, kid. Even with the slow start, you're still the best hitter we have by a longshot. But I don't know, you were connecting with the ball, but you didn't seem to move as fluidly as you normally do up there, so just wanted to check in."

"Thanks, Joe. I'm all good, just a little stiff, and took a few swings to loosen up. Maybe if you guys didn't try to torture us at the start of camp, I wouldn't be quite so stiff."

Joe chuckled. "Where would be the fun in that? Making grown men cry during camp is my greatest pleasure in life. I look forward to it all year."

"That doesn't surprise me at all."

"Make sure you ice if you need to." Joe held his stare for a few seconds, then nodded and headed back to the mound.

Pete rested his bat against the side of the dugout and stepped down the stairs to grab his glove. A new kid was sitting where Pete's glove had been and his glove was on the ground. He bent down and picked it up and pointedly stared at the rookie from Texas State. "I know you're new here, but we try to treat everyone else's equipment the same way we'd treat our own."

"Whatever." The young guy spat his chew on the floor of the dugout.

"Jesus," Pete muttered. "You haven't made the team yet, you'd do well to remember that."

"Oh, I'll make the team, and I'll be knocking you out of your spot in the lineup while I'm at it."

"It's Darren, right?" Pete asked.

Darren nodded. "Yeah."

"Look, Darren, I'm all for being confident. If you make the team, I'd love to see you come gunning for my spot, because if you can catch me that means our team is having a great year on the sticks and that's good for all of us. But there's a big difference between confident, cocky and straight up dick. Trust me when I say you're being a dick and I'm sure that's not what you are going for."

Darren stood up and grabbed his batting glove out of his back pocket and spat on the ground beside Pete's feet. "Thanks for the tip, Pops," he said and walked out of the dugout.

Pete stared at the little punk's back as he walked to the plate. Holy shit, that kid was unreal.

He made his way down the line to Gonzo and Smitty, where they stood waiting for their turn to bat.

"Nice job out there. You looked a little tight at first, but then you started to look more like yourself," Smitty said.

He exhaled. "Getting older sucks. I feel every one of my years when I'm surrounded by these young kids," Pete replied.

"Yeah 'cuz you're such a washed-up has-been at thirty," Smitty laughed.

Pete snickered. "No, definitely not washed up. I'm going to fucking crush it this year, but Jesus, these kids. I swear to god I wasn't an asshole at my first training camp." He glanced over at the kid in question as he lined up to bat.

"What makes you say that?" Gonzo asked.

"What? That I wasn't an asshole, or that these kids are?"

"Take your pick," Gonzo replied.

"I just met that Darren kid." He nodded towards the batting cage. "No respect whatsoever."

"Ah, did the new kid not fawn all over you, Zip?" Gonzo joked.

"Fuck you." Pete laughed. "I couldn't give two shits if anyone fawns over me, but the least he could do is not spit splash my shoes." He glanced down at the shoe in question and rubbed the toe of his shoe with his other foot.

"Man, I still remember my first camp. I was in awe." He shook his head as the memories of what his first camp had been like swarmed back to him. "It took everything in me not to fangirl at being on the field with some of those guys." He sighed. "I'd grown up watching some of them and shit, my first time playing on the big field with them, man..."

"I know what you mean. It seems like a million years ago now, but yeah, I hear you. I made an ass of myself asking for tips and trying to make friends." Smitty snickered. "I went broke paying for drinks and those bastards let me, then bugged the shit out of me all season about it."

"Right? That's what I'm talking about." He nodded towards Darren. "That's not how that kid acted at all. It was weird."

Gonzo shrugged. "Maybe he just shows his nerves differently."

"Or maybe he's just a douche," Pete muttered.

Gonzo snorted. "Yeah, that could be it, too." He clapped Pete on the back. "Guess time will tell."

After practice, Pete made his way back to the locker room. He eyed Ryan lying with his arm in an ice bath and he snickered. "Rough day?"

"I didn't think so, but Jessie thinks otherwise and she's making me ice." Ryan shifted his weight and his body slipped deeper into the tub and he hissed out a breath.

Pete winced in sympathy. There was nothing quite like an ice bath.

"You waiting your turn for the bath, old man?" a voice interrupted.

Pete turned around and his eyes widened when he saw Darren. "What's your problem, kid?"

"Nothing, you're just in my position, that's all."

"Got news for you, Meat. It's not your position till you earn it and there's no way in hell that's happening this season."

"We'll see," Darren blustered.

"Here's the thing, kid. I don't know what things were like where you came from, but here on this team, it's about being a team, a family, having each other's back. Not thinking you are good enough to be a one man show."

"Maybe that's because you aren't as good as you used to be and you need backup," Darren mocked.

Ryan reared back in the ice bath and Pete set his hand on his shoulder. He didn't need support to deal with this little shit.

"Or maybe it's that baseball is a fucking team sport, Meat. Here's a freebie for you. The guys who make it in the Bigs, I mean really make it, know that. They know the value of team, building morale and having each other's backs." Pete glanced at Ryan. A Cy Young winning pitcher who was one of the nicest guys in the sport, his brother for all intents and purposes, and how did he repay him? By sleeping with his sister. Shit, maybe he wasn't the best person to give this little pep talk.

"Yeah, I don't need anyone having my back. Thanks," Darren mocked.

"And you'll be gone before you even make the team with that kind of attitude, Meat." Pete shook his head as he looked at the kid. "It doesn't matter how good a ballplayer you are. If no one wants to play with you, then you won't have a team. And if you don't have a team, you're just a kid with a bat."

"And you're just some old guy who hasn't realized his time is done," Darren replied.

"Jesus, Meat. I'm trying to help you, but come on. You gotta work with me here."

"Why the fuck do you keep calling me Meat?" Darren growled.

Pete glanced at Ryan, and they both laughed. Turning back to Darren, Pete said, "Are you serious? How the hell can you not know the Meat reference? Bull Durham, baby."

"Bull Durham? God, you really are old," Darren scoffed.

"I call it seasoned, thanks, and everyone knows Bull Durham."

"It's true," Ryan agreed. "Freakin' classic. You should watch it, Meat."

"Whatever," Darren sneered.

"Dude, word to the wise. I don't know if you're just used to being the big dog and that's why you're acting all tough, but here, you're not a big dog. You're like a freaking chihuahua. Loud, annoying, and no one is worried about what you can do because we're all bigger and stronger. So, drop the 'tude, or your career will be over before it even begins because I can honestly say with the way you're behaving, I don't know a damn person who would want to play with you."

"Well, you won't have to worry about it when I take your spot."

"Wow, you are unreal." Pete stared down the rookie. The kid had real potential, but his ego and inability to take advice were going to kill his dreams.

Ryan stepped out of the ice bath and wrapped a towel around himself. "I need a beer," Ryan said to Pete.

"Done," Pete agreed.

Ryan stopped beside Darren. "Kid, I don't know what your plan was here, but you fucked up. If you are dumb enough to think you can intimidate him with your attitude, you are dumber than I thought. You're gunning for an infield position and you had the chance to play and learn from one of the best in the league and you threw that away because you wanted to play bigshot." Ryan slapped Darren on the back. "If you want to have any chance at a career, you need to grow the fuck up. Shut your mouth and learn from people who have what you want and can show you how to get there."

"We getting beer?" Gonzo called.

"Absolutely," Pete replied. "We're done here, let's go Ry."

"Smitty, you in?" Gonzo called.

"When am I not?" Smitty hollered back.

Side by side, they walked back to their lockers. "Man, if my ego had been like that when I was his age, my sister would have brained me with my bat." Ryan laughed.

At the mention of Kendall, Pete winced. He was a shitty friend. There was no way Ryan would want to go for beers or be standing up for him if he knew what had happened between him and Kendall. Their friendship would be over. All that stuff he'd just spouted about teamwork and family would be gone too when Ryan refused to play with him. It's a good thing they'd decided not to carry on after she left San Diego. His chest tightened. Why did he want to call her so badly?

Several minutes later, the four men filed into a small pub down the street from the stadium. Pete scanned the bar and spotted an open table in the back corner. He nodded toward it. The bars and restaurants around the stadium were always slammed this time of day. Fans and players alike all seemed to need to unwind after a long day of camp.

"You guys looked good out there already," a voice called to his left. Pete turned towards the person and pulled up short. A smile split across his face when he saw the group of older men sitting at the high-top table with a pitcher of beer and plates full of chicken wings.

"If you guys keep filling up on shit food every time you come down here your wives are going to stop letting you come," Pete said as he walked over to the table and shook hands with the four men. They'd been coming down to spring training for a boys' trip the entire time Pete had played for the Hawks.

"Hey guys, glad to see you were able to come down again this year. I thought you were talking about heading down to Florida this year for spring training to see how the other half lived," Gonzo said.

"Nah, we couldn't abandon you guys. Had to see if this hotshot pitcher you signed needed any tips."

"Hey now, I taught Pete here everything he knows. He was having some trouble hitting me last season, so I thought I should make the move so I don't keep embarrassing him," Ryan joked.

Wrapping his arm around Ryan's neck, Pete aggressively noogied his old friend. "Ha ha." Straightening, he turned Ryan towards the table. "Ry, this is Salty, Mik, Rem and Stu. Guys, meet Ryan Graves."

Salty stood up and shook Ryan's hand. "It's a real honor to meet you, Ryan. I've followed your career. We're real lucky to have you here."

"Thank you, sir. I'm thrilled to be here."

"World Series, baby," Mik called out and threw up his hands for his friends to high-five.

"Let's not get ahead of ourselves." Smitty laughed.

"Ahead of ourselves? It's a given. You guys made it to the National League finals last year and that was with the crappy pitching you had," Rem said.

"We didn't have crappy pitching." Pete rolled his eyes.

"Well, you didn't have this guy pitching for you," Salty pointed his thumb towards Ryan. "We're expecting big things outta you boys this year."

"We'll do our best," Pete said and patted Salty on the back. "It's good to see you guys." He pushed past them and they claimed the last remaining table in the pub.

They'd barely sat down when the owner's wife Yvette stopped at their table. "Hey guys, good to have you back. You want a jug?"

"Absolutely," Smitty replied. "Good to see you, Vettie. This is our new guy, Ryan."

"Ah, the pitcher everyone is talking about." She looked Ryan up and down. "You as good as they say you are?"

"Here's hoping," Ryan replied.

Yvette grinned. "You'll do. I was expecting you to be like some of these other cocky guys around here. Should have known when you came in with these three you wouldn't be, but I wanted to see for myself. Glad to meet you."

"Geesh, I didn't know I'd be put through the ringer going for beer with you guys," Ryan said.

"What can we say? We're fan favorites," Gonzo joked. "You want to hang with the big dogs, you gotta walk the talk." Gonzo looked at Pete and winked. "You see what I did with the big dogs there?"

Pete snorted at the bad joke. "Yeah, I got it, real clever." He leaned back in his chair. He'd missed this during the offseason. Sure, he'd hung out with the guys and worked out, but it was different grabbing a beer after practice during the season when the hum of the game was buzzing all around you. Seeing Ryan here with Pete's best friends from the team and how well he fit in, it was like the last piece of the puzzle clicked into place. Salty and the guys were right. Now that they had Ryan here they stood a chance of winning the World Series.

He meshed well with the guys and having a team that jelled was a huge part of winning.

"How'd it go with my sister?" Ryan asked, breaking Pete out of thoughts. He winced. Shit, if Ryan knew just how well things had gone with Kendall, any hope they had of the team running like a well-oiled machine went right out the window.

"It went good. Her work kept her pretty busy."

"Hang on, back up, what do you mean how'd it go with your sister?" Gonzo asked.

Ryan scowled over at him. "Not like that, asshole. Pete gave her a place to crash because I was already down here."

"How old is she?" Smitty asked.

"Twenty-seven," Ryan replied. "Why?"

"What's she look like?" Smitty waggled his eyebrows.

"None of your business, "Ryan snarled. "That's my fucking sister, asshole."

Smitty winced. "I was just kidding."

"Why was she in town?" Gonzo asked.

Pete glanced at Gonzo. What the hell was with the twenty questions?

"She had to be there for work," Pete replied.

"Huh, and she couldn't stay in a hotel?" Gonzo pursed his mouth and nodded his head like that was the most interesting thing he'd ever heard.

"Why would she waste a bunch of money staying in a hotel when she could stay with Pete for free?" Ryan asked.

"Wouldn't her work pay for her to be there if they want her there?" Gonzo again questioned.

"I don't know," Ryan replied. "She asked me if she could stay with me. I told her I was out of town and suggested she call Zip since she's known him forever." Ryan shrugged. "Who wants to stay in a hotel when you can stay with a friend and not be alone all the time? It sucks enough going to a strange city for work without having to spend your evening by yourself, too."

Pete breathed a sigh of relief at Ryan's response. Thank god Ryan had fielded the question because he was pretty sure if he'd answered, he would have come up with some lame excuse that would have made it clear to everyone exactly how they spent Kendall's down time. He glanced over at Ryan.

God, he was such a shitty friend.

"My sister is pretty cool though, hey?" Ryan asked.

Pete swallowed past the lump in his throat. That was putting it mildly. "Yeah, it was fun hanging out with her as adults." Pete winced. Crap, why did he say it like that? He glanced over at Ryan to see if he noticed, but he was scanning the bar like nothing was out of the ordinary, and Pete breathed a sigh of relief. Time to change the subject. "You guys see any rooks or walk-ons who looked promising?"

"I would have said that Darren kid until he opened his fucking mouth. But my god," Gonzo grumbled.

"Yeah, if Coach asks like he normally does, that one will be a big no for me," Smitty replied.

"Your coach asks what you think of the new guys?" Ryan asked.

"Yeah, usually. He will usually sit the infielders all together to talk about some of the prospects and what our concerns are about them, what we liked, what we didn't like." Pete shrugged. "He doesn't always go with who we want, but he always listens and takes it into consideration."

"Yeah, I'd say that kid would be better off trying out for a different team because I'd be shocked if Coach picks him based on everyone not wanting him," Gonzo replied. "That was some weird shit. Who does that on day one?"

"I'll probably talk to Coach about him tomorrow morning, so he knows what we're all thinking. I don't want him wasting a bunch of time watching him if we're all going to veto him, anyway."

"That's cool that Coach asks you. I've never had a coach really care what the players think."

"Yeah, he's pretty big on team building and family and all that shit like Zip said," Smitty replied.

"Nice. I'm really looking forward to seeing that in action and playing for him," Ryan said.

Yvette dropped the pitcher of beer down on the table with four glasses. "You boys want anything to eat?"

"Yeah, can we get four burgers?" Pete asked.

Yvette eyed them all skeptically. "You sure you boys all want that? Maybe I should bring you something with some vegetables."

"Don't worry, I'll be going for a run tonight so I can keep my boyish figure." Pete winked at her.

"Well, I have to look out for your female fans. Right now, you fill out that uniform pretty nicely." She eyed Gonzo. "I'm bringing you a salad."

"Ouch." He laughed and placed his hand on his stomach. "Okay, yeah, maybe salad is a good call."

Pete snickered as he looked at Gonzo pressing his fingers against his abdomen. "Dude, stop being such a girl. You look fine."

"Says Mr. Six-Pack. Not all of us have your genes, Zip," Gonzo grumbled.

"Dad bods are in right now. You're fine," Smitty snickered.

"Fuck you, I don't have a dad bod." Gonzo reached over and punched Smitty hard on the arm.

"Ouch."

"I'm going for a run with you tonight, Zip," Gonzo grumbled.

"All right, sweetheart. We'll get you back down to fighting weight," Pete teased.

Man, he really had missed this. It was going to be a great season. This was going to be their year. World Series, here we come.

CHAPTER EIGHT

K endall held her skirt down with her hands as she slid onto the bench seat across from her friend Samantha. She glanced at the server and smiled. "I'm going to need a glass of white wine. The biggest one you can find."

"That kind of day, I see," Sam murmured

"Don't even get me started." She reached across the table and squeezed her hand. "It's good to see you."

"You too, girl. I missed you. Two weeks is a long time."

The server set the glass of wine down in front of Kendall. She picked it up and took a sip. Closing her eyes, she held it in her mouth to savor the flavor for a moment, then slowly swallowed.

"Wow, you weren't kidding about what kind of day you've had."

Kendall set the glass down on the table. "No, it was a bit of a bitch. The pile on my desk didn't decrease at all while I was away. In fact, I think it had babies."

"Ah, you'll knock it back down in no time. No one is better at all that time management crap than you."

"Thank you, but I think it will take more than time management to wrangle it into submission." Kendall leaned forward and rested her elbows on the table. "So tell me, what's been going on here since I left?"

"Uh-uh, no chance. You sent all those cryptic texts about Pete, so dish. I want all the dirty details."

She shrugged. "There's not much to tell. I live here, he lives there, end of story."

"No, no, no." Sam shook her head. "You're not getting off that easy. Saying end of story implies there's a story, so come on." She held up her hands in the universal come here sign. "Give it to me. And don't leave anything out, Momma's had a dry spell. I need to live vicariously."

Kendall dropped her head on the table and groaned. "I'm an idiot."

Sam stroked the back of her head. "Why are you an idiot?"

Picking up her head, she peeked up at her closest friend. "Because I fell in love with Pete."

"I thought you already were in love with Pete. I thought that was the whole point of staying with him to exorcise him through sex."

"Turns out I was only half in love with him before I left. Now I'm all the way." She dropped her head back down on the table. "I think I was better off before," she whined.

"The sex was that good, huh?"

Kendall sat up straight and looked at her friend across the table. "It was better than that."

"Oh god, spill," Sam squealed.

"He's just...god." Kendall shifted in her chair and took a sip of her wine. How did she put into words what being with Pete was like? "He's even better than I remember. When we were younger, he was this hotshot, cocky player."

Sam raised her eyebrow. "And you liked that?"

"Um, have you seen the man? Yes, I liked that. But now he's...I don't know, he's sweet and caring and..." She sighed. "He's so much sexier than I remembered."

"I'm not seeing the problem."

"The problem is, it was supposed to just be a fling. We'd fuck each other's brains out and go on our merry way."

A sad smile clipped the corner of Sam's lips. "But you can't go on your merry way?"

"No," Kendall groaned. "God, why was I dumb enough to think I could? I'm not a casual sex kind of girl." Sam snickered, making Kendall roll her eyes. "Well, I am, but not with guys I actually like. Why did I think I could be with someone I've been half in love with since I was twelve years old?"

"I'm guessing because you were hoping he'd finally feel the same way about you."

Tears burned behind Kendall's eyes. *Dammit.* "This is so stupid. I knew going into this what would happen. He was really clear on all the reasons why this couldn't go anywhere." She looked up at the ceiling and blinked rapidly to hold the tears at bay. "I don't know why I was so naïve to think he didn't really mean it." She sighed. "I don't know. I guess some stupid part of me was hoping we'd have the time together and suddenly he'd look at me and realize he'd always loved me and we'd live happily ever after."

Sam smiled sadly at her. "How would that work, though, really? He lives in San Diego and you live here. It's not like you could have a real relationship with that much distance between you."

"Why not? People do it all the time," Kendall complained.

"People, yes. You? No." Sam looked at her with the knowing eyes of a friend who had been through the trenches with her and knew where the bodies were buried.

"Yeah, you're right. I guess I just figured after all this time he wouldn't live up to the hype." She picked up her glass of wine and took a sip. "I mean, he's a professional athlete. They are known for being womanizing assholes." She pursed her lips as she met Sam's knowing stare. "I figured he'd probably suck in bed because he never had to bother with learning how to pleasure a woman because there was always another one waiting around the corner."

"I take it he didn't suck?"

"No. The sex was like..." She paused. "It was like the shit sonnets are written about. We're talking rockets going off, furniture breaking, can barely walk the next day kind of sex."

Sam whistled. "Damn."

"Yeah, that's not the kind of thing that makes you want to pack up and move on. And then to top it all off, he had me go with him to this low-income housing thing he wants to start up and fuck," she growled. "Could he be more perfect for me?"

"Did you talk to him about how you're feeling?"

"What?" She gaped at her friend. "Are you crazy? There is no way I was going to tell him how crazy I am about him when he just kept talking about our expiration date."

"Maybe he felt the same way and just didn't tell you?" Sam suggested hopefully.

"I wish, but no. He was really clear that as great as our time together was, we didn't have a future. Mostly because of my brother."

"Screw your brother. He doesn't get to have a say in your love life."

"No, but he does get to have a say if my love life involves one of his best friends."

Annoyed, Sam waved her arm and made a scoffing noise. "Maybe when you were in high school, sure. But now? Why would he care?"

"I don't know, something about team dynamics and being in sync with each other or some such nonsense."

Sam's head cocked to the side as she stared at her. Kendall fought not to squirm in her chair. "What?"

"Maybe you should tell him how you feel. He'd be an idiot not to want to be with you once he knows."

There was no way she was doing that. Everything in her told her it wouldn't end the way she wanted it to. Pete had made it clear to her how much his friendship with Ryan and the team meant to him. There was no way he'd risk it after a week with her. Besides, no one ever chose her over her brother. This wouldn't be any different, but it sure would hurt more. "No, we agreed to what this was. I'm not going to try to change the terms now. This way, I have some great memories and no one really got hurt. We can both walk away and move on with our lives."

"Are you sure you can do that?" Sam asked.

Kendall flipped her hair away from her face and sighed. "I'm going to have to."

Sam stared at her for several moments, then seeming to come to some conclusion, she nodded her head. "All right then, 'Operation Forget Pete' is now in effect."

"What the hell is 'Operation Forget Pete'?"

"We're getting you back out there dating ASAP so you can find someone better."

"Yeah, I'm not sure I'm quite there yet, Sam."

Pinning her with a stare, Sam leaned back in her chair. The look of determination on her face made Kendall shudder. Great, she'd seen that look before. There was no way she was getting out of this one.

"And we are starting with the two guys at the bar who've been staring at us for the past twenty minutes."

Kendall glanced over to the bar where two twenty-something men in designer suits sat casually glancing over their way. She turned back to Sam. "I don't know Sam. I'm not really—"

"Nope, end of discussion. You've pined over that man long enough. If he wants you, he knows how to find you. Until then, we are going to find you a man who knows what a good thing he has in front of him." Sam glanced over at the bar and waved the two men over. "Starting now."

"Lord help me," she complained.

Moments later, the two men arrived at their table carrying drinks in each hand. "May we?" the taller of the two asked.

"Please," Sam replied, gesturing for them to sit.

Suit number two sat down beside Kendall and slid a glass of wine in front of her. "I believe this is what you are drinking," he said, like he'd just presented her with her favorite type of cookie or something rather than a glass of generic white wine. His gaze slid down her body familiarly, lingering on her cleavage and a slight smirk slid across his face.

Gross. She eyed the drink in front of her. Seeing the creepy leer on his face, there was zero chance she was drinking that. "Thanks, but sorry, I don't take drinks from strange men." Kendall smiled to soften the blow.

"Oh, come on, don't tell me you're one of those girls."

Kendall's spine stiffened at the implied insult. "What kind of girls are those? The ones who don't like to be roofied? Yeah, I am one of those girls."

"That's not what he meant," suit number one said, trying to come to the rescue.

"It sure as hell sounded like it." She glanced over at Sam and flashed her a look as if to say, really? You've got to be kidding me. Sam grimaced and mouthed sorry. "Thanks, guys, but you can take your drinks and find some other people to enjoy them with. We made a mistake asking you to join us."

"Bitch," suit number two snarled as he grabbed the drinks from the table and slid off the bench.

Holy shit, with guys like that, there was zero chance she'd ever get over Pete.

"Okay, so we need a do-over. That doesn't count towards the operation. That one's for the blooper reel," Sam said. "Sorry, they looked so normal. Who'd have thought they'd be such douches?"

"Unfortunately, they often are," Kendall muttered.

"Come on, they aren't usually that bad." Sam glanced around the bar and scowled. "Maybe we need to start closer to home. Have I ever told you about Simon from my work?"

Oh, good god. Kendall groaned. She had unleashed a monster. This was going to be worse than she'd imagined. She flicked her hand up to catch the server's eye. They were going to need more drinks.

His phone rang. Glancing at the screen, he saw Kendall's name. Pete grabbed his earbuds and put them in as he hit answer.

"Hey, how are you?"

"I'm good. How are you doing? How's camp going?"

"It's going. Are you back home now or are you still in San Diego?"

"No, I'm home now. That's why I'm calling. I wanted to let you know that you no longer have a squatter in your place."

"I'd hardly call you a squatter."

"Well, when you get home, you'll have the place all to yourself."

His stomach clenched at the idea of going home and not seeing her there. What the hell was that about? He was being ridiculous. He was just worried about Mooch, that's all. "How was Mooch before you left?"

"Well, let's just say I think he's a little annoyed at you and I'm sure he will be even more so when you get back."

"Why do you say he's annoyed?" he asked.

"Umm, he might have sprayed the side of your couch?"

"Sprayed it with what?" he asked.

Kendall's snicker cut through the line, and he sat up straighter on the bed. "Why are you laughing? Did he take a piss on my couch?"

"No, he didn't pee exactly. He just did that spray thing cats do."

"What the fuck is a spray thing cats do?"

Kendall giggled again. "They just sort of lift their tails and spray?"

"What the fuck? Like a skunk."

"Kind of," she giggled again.

"Jesus," he muttered. "I can just imagine what I'll come home to then."

"It'll be fine. You have that pet sitter coming in starting tomorrow. She called a couple times this week and came by for coffee to get Mooch more comfortable with her. She's very sweet. I think everything will be fine."

"It better be," he grumbled. "Or he'll be finding new accommodations."

"All right, tough guy, kick him to the curb if he gets up to any funny business." Kendall teased.

"You laugh, but I will."

"Sure you will."

"Okay, I probably won't but that doesn't mean he won't get a stern talking to about not shitting where he eats and spraying my furniture falls in that category."

"Fair enough. So how was your day? How's camp going" she asked.

"It's going pretty good. My hitting was off the first couple of days, which sucked. This dipshit rookie kid they've got at camp is a cocky little fucker who seems to think he'll be sliding into my spot this season, so that's always fun."

"How was your fielding?"

"It was good." He pictured the snag he'd made that he'd managed to rifle into a double play. No way the rookie would have gotten to that ball. "The little fucker isn't taking my position."

Kendall laughed. "Sounds like you're making friends."

He snorted. "I have enough friends." He leaned back on the couch and rested his feet on the coffee table. "Ryan said you and your friends are coming to our game in Atlanta for the season opener."

"Yeah, my girlfriends have never been to a professional game, so it should be fun."

"Tell me about them." He settled back on the couch and propped the pillow up behind his neck to get more comfortable.

"You really want me to talk about my friends with you?"

"Yeah. We're friends, right?"

"I thought you had enough friends."

He scrubbed his hand across his head. He didn't want to just be friends with her. Talking to her was dangerous. The easy way they talked, just hearing her voice at the end of the day quieted something inside him he hadn't realized was noisy until this moment.

"I don't know, Ken. It's just nice to hear your voice."

"It's nice to hear yours, too. But I thought we agreed we weren't going to do this. That we were just going to let it be what it was. We had a great week together, made some memories and that's all it can be."

"Yeah, no, it doesn't make sense to drag this out at all. You're right. And it's not like anything can happen when I'm in town with your brother there, so there's really no place for this to go, anyway." He dropped his head back. Just because it made sense didn't mean it didn't suck.

Silence filled the air, with neither of them speaking. Finally, Kendall spoke up. "So my friends Samantha, Jenna and Theresa will come with me."

"How'd you meet them?"

"Sam and I met during our undergrad degrees. We were in a gender studies class together."

"What does that have to do with marketing?"

"I needed an arts credit, and it sounded interesting. Besides, understanding people and society, who people are and what makes them tick is all part of marketing. It was actually really useful even though originally when I signed up, I just thought it seemed like an easy credit."

"Is that Sam's field?"

"Sort of. She's a lawyer, specializing in women's issues and gender equality."

"Wow."

"Yeah, and Jenna works with her at the same law firm, but she's in corporate law."

"What about Theresa?"

"She's a psychologist."

"Jesus," he muttered. He'd barely graduated from high school and Kendall's best friends were freaking lawyers and doctors. It had never been more clear just how different their lives were. She was so far out of his league.

"They've never slummed it at a ball game, huh?"

"Nope, they don't know what they are missing out on," she needled. "I think they're going to love it. I mean, how can they not? All those cute guys in ball-pants."

"You better not be looking at all the guys."

"I'm just looking at one," she murmured.

Shit. That's why this was a bad idea. The chemistry between him and Kendall was unreal and ultimately always led back to this. He cleared his throat.

"It was good talking to you. I'm glad you made it home safe."

"It was good talking to you, too. Thanks again for letting me crash with you."

"No problem."

He didn't want to hang up the phone and stop talking to her, but continuing on was pointless. "Bye Ken."

"Bye Pete."

He pushed the button to hang up his phone and tossed it onto the couch beside him. Unwilling to sit around and sulk, he scooped his phone back up and hit Gonzo's number. The second he picked up, he said, "I'm ready to run. Meet me downstairs in five."

Gonzo groaned on the other end of the line. "If you aren't there, I'm going without you," Pete snarled.

CHAPTER NINE

K endall pulled open her front door and shook her head when she saw her best friend. "Oh my god, Sam, you look like you got thrown up on by the fan club." She scanned Sam's body and her eyes widened when she looked at her socks.

"No." Kendall shook her head as she continued to stare at the offensive display. "There is no way you are wearing all that shit to the game. You look ridiculous."

Samantha looked at her feet. "What's wrong with them?"

"You have my brother's face on your socks." She shook her head again. "That's just wrong on so many levels." She placed her hands on her hips. "You have to pick. Everything on your body can't be fan gear. It's just too much."

The doorbell rang again. "If you're keeping the socks, then you're changing your shorts. Where the hell did you find spandex shorts that look like baseball pants, anyway?"

She pulled open the door and groaned when she saw what greeted her on the other side. Jenna and Theresa weren't any better than Sam. In fact, it looked like they'd all planned their outfits together. When they'd decided to do a girls' day watching baseball, she'd assumed her friends had at least seen a game before. Their outfits said otherwise.

"Why the hell do you all have socks with my brother's face on them?"

Jenna laughed. "Because it's funny." She reached into her purse and pulled out a pair for Kendall.

"There is no way I'm wearing those."

The three women stood side-by-side and struck a pose, making Kendall groan again. "Disgusting. It's like my brother's fan club threw up on you all." Turning on her heel, she walked to her bedroom.

"Where are you going?" Theresa yelled.

"I'm changing." She took off her Graves jersey and tossed it on her bed. She ran her hands over the Saunders jersey Pete had given her and slipped it on her body. When she'd gotten dressed earlier, she hadn't dared to wear Pete's jersey because her brother would be all over her, but with the way her friends were dressed, she could easily get away with it.

Kendall walked out of the bedroom and rounded the corner to the living room. Three faces smirked back at her.

"Haha, told ya," Sam said. "Pay up." She held out her hand palm up to Theresa.

"What's going on?" Kendall asked.

"I told her if we went all out on Ryan gear, you'd wear Pete's jersey to the game today," Sam gloated.

Kendall narrowed her eyes as she looked at her friends. "How'd you know I'd do that?"

"Because you are nothing if not predictable. You hate feeding into your brother's ego, so there was no way you were going to wear something with his name on it if we all looked this ridiculous." Sam wrapped her arm around her shoulder. "Besides, I knew you needed an excuse to wear Pete's jersey, so we thought we'd help you out with that."

"Thanks, guys." She looked at the three of them standing together in their gear. "You do realize you have to go out afterwards looking like that, right?"

"Ah, we've worn worse. Besides, it'll be like Halloween," Sam said.

At the stadium, they passed their tickets to be scanned and strolled up the stairs to the first level.

"Where are our seats?" Jenna asked.

"We are on this level on the third base line," Kendall replied.

"I have no idea where that is, so we'll just follow you." Theresa linked arms with Kendall. "Lead the way, captain."

"Let's grab a beer first," Kendall replied.

Sam wrinkled her nose, and Kendall held up her hand. "Nope, it's non-negotiable. You're at the ball field, you drink beer. Period. I won't make you eat a hot dog, but you are going to drink beer." She stepped into the line behind a couple of Atlanta fans.

The men turned around and looked at the women. "I think you got your jerseys mixed up, girls. This is Atlanta.

The home team jersey looks like this." The heavyset man picked his shirt away from his chest to indicate the home team logo.

"Oh, shoot, thanks for telling us. Bless your heart," Kendall laid on her fake southern accent and batted her eyelashes at the neanderthal in front of her.

She looked at her friends and rolled her eyes. "And that is why we are all having beer."

Theresa flicked her chocolate brown hair off her shoulder and stood up taller. "They might be the home team, but Atlanta is going down tonight. Graves is going to pitch a no-hitter," she taunted the big man in front of them.

"Sure he is, sweetheart," the man mocked. "It takes more than pretty uniforms to win ballgames."

"Yeah, it takes skill and the Hawks have that," Theresa declared.

"Next," the kid behind the counter called out and Kendall slid over to his till.

"Can I grab four beers, please?"

She paid for the drinks and handed one to each of her friends. Kendall led the way down to their seats. She'd grown up watching baseball and loved everything about it. The atmosphere in the stadium, the crack when the bat hit the ball, that first sip of a crisp cold stadium beer. Perfection. It wasn't America's pastime for nothing.

"This is exciting," Jenna said from beside her.

"There's nothing like your first live ballgame." Kendall smiled.

Theresa leaned in front of Jenna. "It's called a no-hitter, right?"

"Yep, it is."

"So then, why did that guy make fun of me like that?"

Lord, her friends were so sweet. Clueless about baseball, but sweet. They couldn't care less about the game and were only here because she wanted to come.

"No-hitter's are pretty rare. It's one thing to say the Hawks are going to win, another thing to say it'll be a no-hitter."

"Shoot, I thought I had this all down pat. I read all the rules last night so I wouldn't have to ask a bunch of stupid questions and did, anyway."

Kendall reached across Jenna and squeezed Theresa's hand. "It wasn't stupid at all and I really appreciate the effort." She glanced at all three women. "Thanks for coming. It means a lot to me. If you have any questions, ask. You'll have a lot more fun if you get involved."

The atmosphere in the stadium shifted as the visiting team came out onto the field.

Kendall jumped up. "Wooo let's go Hawks," she yelled as loud as she could.

Ever since she was a kid, she'd stayed standing until her brother looked over at her and gave her the nod. It didn't take long before Ryan glanced up at her, smiled, and touched the brim of his hat. Out of the corner of her eye, she saw Pete turn towards the stands. Her gaze met his and even from this distance, she swore she could feel the heat from his stare. She raised her hand and gave him a small wave, and his lips curved up in a crooked smile that made her stomach flip. He held her stare for a couple more seconds, then turned and threw the ball to first to continue his warmup.

Kendall dropped down into her seat and sighed. Her reaction to Pete was unreal. She had to get it together before she saw him after the game, otherwise there was no way her brother wouldn't think something was up with them.

"Damn," Sam murmured. "That's hot."

"What's hot?"

"That eye fuck that just happened between you and number 7 down there. I assume that's Pete," Sam asked.

"We didn't just eye fuck," Kendall muttered. Although it sure felt like they did.

"Um, yeah, you did." Jenna waved her hand in front of herself to fan her face. "Very hot. The player and the eye fucking." Jenna waggled her eyebrows.

"He is ridiculously hot." She took a sip of her beer. Too bad they'd agreed the smart thing was just to be friends.

In the bottom of the sixth, Pete walked out of the dugout and stood on deck. He glanced up to where they were sitting and their eyes connected. She smiled. He tipped his head down and took a couple of practice swings. What was that about? During the game, her brother was always so laser focused he didn't even remember his family was there. What did it mean that Pete not only remembered she was there, he'd searched the crowd to see her?

"Oh my god," Jenna squealed and grabbed her arm.

Kendall's heart raced as Pete lined up in the batter's box. The bases were loaded. The first pitch flew across the plate. Strike. Damn. She took a deep breath and willed him to smash the ball. The second pitch was outside. Ball.

She held her breath as the third pitch sailed towards the plate. Crack. The bat connected to the ball and sent it flying deep over the left field fence.

Kendall jumped up and screamed as Pete jogged around the bases. Holy shit, a grand slam! He stepped across home plate and as he walked back to the dugout he looked up at her again and tipped his hat.

Her heart fluttered in her chest. How the hell was she supposed to want to just be friends when he found a way to include her in a moment like that?

"Nice game, boys," Ryan said as he dropped onto the bench beside Pete and started undoing his shoes.

"Where are we meeting up with your sister and her friends?" Jeff Smith said as he sat down beside Ryan on the bench.

"Who said you were coming out to meet my sister?" Ryan asked.

"Pete said your sister was at the game with her friends," Jeff replied.

"Yeah, what was up with you tipping your hat to my sister after your big hit?"

Pete shrugged. That probably hadn't been his best idea, but he was stoked about the grand slam and wanted to see her face. "She was talking trash about my batting when she was in town, so..." He stopped talking, hoping Ryan would just let it go.

"That still doesn't explain why you looked up at her. You could have trash talked her back later." Ryan shifted in his chair so he was facing Pete. "It's kind of weird you even thought to look up at her."

Crap. Pete swallowed. What was he supposed to say about that?

"It's kind of hard not to see her and her friends when they jump around in Hawks' gear in the sea of red. It probably just caught his eye," Ramon Gonzalez said from his cubby in front of them. "They kind of stood out in that crowd."

"No kidding," Pete laughed. He breathed a sigh of relief. Thank god for Gonzo. He'd dodged a bullet there.

"You gonna let Smitty and I join you guys?" Gonzo asked.

"If I let you come, my sister is off limits."

"Why, is she married or something?" Gonzo peeled off his shirt and pants and grabbed his towel off the hook.

"No, but she's too good for the likes of you guys. She's not a groupie, she's a relationship girl," Ryan answered.

Pete's stomach knotted at the reminder that Kendall was too good for him. He was the product of a broken home with a piece of shit dad, he'd barely graduated highschool and life had taught him relationships never last. And like Ryan said, she was a forever kind of girl, despite her protests otherwise. He couldn't offer her anything. They lived in completely different states, for god's sake. If he was smart, he wouldn't even go tonight, but he wanted to see her. Even though he shouldn't.

Pete stood up and pulled his clothes off and tossed them in the hamper as he made his way to the shower. While the water pounded down on his head, he tried to talk himself out of the way he was feeling about seeing Kendall again. She was Ryan's sister. Yeah, they'd had a hot few days together, but they'd both agreed it didn't mean anything. That it couldn't go anywhere. So why the hell had his heart pounded when he'd seen her in the stands tonight?

After the shower, they strolled out of the locker room to find Kendall and her friends leaning against the wall in the hallway with the other wives and girlfriends. Pete's chest tightened as he looked at her. Their eyes connected and for a fleeting instant, he wondered if this was what it felt like when your person was there waiting for you after a game. But then Ryan stepped forward and picked her up and the moment was lost.

Damn, even though she wasn't there for him, he liked walking out and seeing her there. He needed to remember she could never really be his. He was a temporary kind of guy and she was a forever girl.

Conscious of Ryan standing beside him, he gave Kendall a quick hug. "Still think I'm overrated?" he asked.

Kendall looked him up and down and a mischievous smile curled up her lips. "Eh, I mean come on, one good hit." She shrugged.

He laughed. "And 2 RBI's, but who's counting?" He bumped her with his hip. "Can always count on you to keep the ego in check, Ken."

"You know it," she teased. "That's why you guys keep me around."

"What the fuck are you wearing?" Ryan growled.

And for the first time, Pete noticed the number on Kendall's chest. Holy shit, she was wearing his jersey. He couldn't help the smile that broke out across his face. It shouldn't feel that good to have her wearing his jersey, but it did.

Kendall pointed at her friends. "I figured they had your fan club covered. I didn't want you to get a fat head."

Pete glanced at her friends and winced. "Wow, that's a lot of Hawks' gear. I didn't think you could even find that much stuff here."

"Oh, we couldn't find anything locally. We had to order it all online," Kendall's blonde friend said.

"What the hell is that on your socks?" he asked. They looked like little faces.

"It's Ryan's face." Kendall grinned.

"Jesus," Ryan muttered. "Where the hell did you find those?"

"We had them made," Sam beamed at him, making Pete laugh.

"I'm Pete," he said and stuck out his hand.

"Oh, sorry," Kendall replied. "Jenna, Sam and Theresa, this is Pete and this guy over here is my brother, Ryan, but you already know that from the socks." She turned towards his teammates. "Sorry I know who you are but we've never met."

"This is Gonzo and Smitty," Ryan replied. "Guys, this is my sister and her friends."

Ryan wrapped his arm around Kendall's shoulder. "All right, where are we heading?"

"There's a pretty cool bar just about a five-minute walk from your hotel that I thought we could go to. It'll be way less busy than anything down here, that way we can actually hang out and talk."

"Okay, we'll get a ride back to the hotel with the team if you want to meet us in the lobby," Ryan said.

Pete strolled down the bus steps and his eyes immediately landed on Kendall sitting on a bench in front of the hotel.

"You might want to roll your tongue back in your mouth if you don't want Ryan to know you've got a thing for his little sister." Gonzo's voice quietly interrupted his thoughts.

"What? I don't have a thing for Kendall," Pete denied.

"Okay, man, whatever you say." Gonzo raised an eyebrow at him. "But the drool on your chin says otherwise. "

Shit. He really should bow out and just say he was tired and head up to his room.

As they walked towards the building, the women all stood up. Kendall's gaze met his and she smiled. The secret twinkle in her eye as she looked at him reminded him of tangled sheets and hot sex. Who was he kidding? There was no way he was going up to his room.

He pushed his hair back from his forehead. But he could be cool. He was a freaking professional athlete. He knew how to be chill and not let emotions interfere with things. He could go to the pub with Kendall and hang out with her without it being a big deal. She flicked a glance at him and smiled coyly, and his dick twitched. Now he just needed to get his little brain on board with his big. Damn thing had a mind of its own. He shoved his hands in his pocket and winced. That'll teach it who's boss.

"Just give us a minute to run our gear up to the room and we'll be right back," Ryan told the women.

"No problem," Kendall replied.

CHAPTER TEN

Pete dumped his bag in his room and wandered back towards the elevator before meeting Ryan and Gonzo in the hallway. By the time the elevator arrived, Smitty had joined them.

"So, are your sister's friends single?" Smitty asked.

"No idea," Ryan replied.

"Last I heard they were all single," Pete replied.

"How would you know?" Ryan asked.

Pete shrugged. "I don't know. Ken and I talked about her friends when she was at my place, and she mentioned they were all single."

"I'm kind of surprised you talked about that kind of thing," Ryan replied.

Leaning back against the elevator wall, he glanced at the numbers as they descended. "Why wouldn't we talk about that kind of thing? Her friends are important to her."

"Yeah, I know, you just usually don't get that deeply into conversation with a woman to get to know about her friends," Ryan said.

Pete's back stiffened at the dig from his friend. That once again reminded him he wasn't good enough for Kendall. He grit his teeth. "She stayed at my place for a week. I'm not a complete fucking idiot. I can hold a conversation with a woman despite the fact I don't have some fancy degree."

"Woah, what the hell?" Ryan quipped.

The doors to the elevator opened and Pete stalked out towards the group of women. Ryan grabbed his arm. "What was that about?" Ryan asked.

Real cool. Way to keep things under the radar. Pete shook his head. "Nothing, forget about it. I don't know what my problem is."

"You sure?"

"Yeah, it's cool. Just tired, I guess." Pete brushed him off. "Let's go get a beer."

The women stood when they approached. "All right, you ready?" Kendall asked.

"Lead the way," Ryan replied.

Ryan fell in to step with Kendall and Pete dropped back with Gonzo following behind at the back of the group. He mentally chastised himself when his gaze dropped to her ass for the third time.

"What's with you tonight?" Gonzo asked.

"Nothing... I'm just in my own head tonight for some reason."

"Well, I'm here if you need to talk, you know that."

"Yeah, I do, thanks. But I'm fine, really."

They followed Kendall's friends into a neighborhood bar. Pete glanced around. The place was busy, but not wall to wall like the bars near the stadium. Much more in line with the mood he was in this evening. He really didn't have it in him to make small talk with fans.

Jenna wove the group through the bar toward the back where two high-tops sat side-by-side. When she stopped at the first table, she began moving chairs back. "Let's shove these together," she said.

Smitty pushed the two tables together. Pete made eye contact with Kendall. "I'm going to head to the bar and grab some beer," he said.

"I'll come help you," Kendall replied.

They wove their way back toward the bar. While they waited for the bartender, Pete rested his back against the bar top and faced Kendall. "You look good," he murmured.

She cocked her hip against the bar stool. "So do you." She smiled. "You played well tonight."

"Thanks." He clenched his hands into fists so he wouldn't reach out and pull her against him. These feelings he had for her didn't make sense. Normally, when he slept with a woman, he could take or leave hooking up with her again. But Kendall? He'd honestly thought he'd have had his fill of her during their week together, but as he stood here looking at her now, there was nothing he wanted more than to take her back to his hotel room.

"It was cool watching you play. I haven't watched you play live since high school when you and Ry played together."

"Watching me live? Meaning you watch me on TV?"

"I might have watched you every now and then."

"Not just when I was playing against your brother?"

She ducked her head down and he could see her cheeks turning pink. Interesting. Kendall had followed his career. She'd never let on when they'd talked about it before.

He caught the bartender's eye. The man stopped in front of them. "What can I get you?"

Turning to Kendall, Pete asked, "What do your friends like?"

"Can we get a pitcher of margaritas, please, with 4 glasses?"

"Sure, iced or frozen?"

"Frozen, thanks."

"Anything else?" the bartender asked.

"Yeah, I don't know what you have on tap, so can I grab a pitcher of pale ale, but not IPA and 4 glasses as well?"

While they waited for the bartender to get their drinks, Pete turned back to Kendall. "It's really good to see you. I'm glad you came tonight."

"Me too." Kendall glanced over at their group, then turned and smiled shyly at him. "Is this weird for you, too?"

"Little bit." He sighed. "But mostly because I can't touch you like I want to."

"I wish you could too," she replied. She licked her lips and he followed the movement with his gaze. Damn, he wanted to kiss her.

The bartender walked back over to them and set glasses on the bar top, interrupting their conversation. Probably for the best. Standing this close to Kendall made him want things he couldn't have. He stepped back, putting a bit of space between them. "How's work been since you came home?"

"Crazy, but good."

"Were you able to get everything worked out in San Diego before you left?"

"Umm, yes and no. Legal is still sorting out all the legalities so they can fire him because my bosses are done with him. He just finished sensitivity training and is back at work, but I'm not sure how well things are going in the office now that Mark is back. I gave him lots of suggestions. I'm just not sure if he's willing to take them."

"Why not? You know your stuff. I'd think he'd be open to doing what he could to make the office a success."

"Yeah, well, not every man is that good at taking direction from a woman." She rolled her eyes.

"But aren't your bosses here all women?"

"Yep, but he's never worked for them directly. He had rave reviews from his former employer, but he was a man, so it never really occurred to any of them that it might be an issue."

"What an idiot," Pete griped. "A good idea is a good idea."

Kendall smiled. "Not everyone has that same opinion,"

"Well, people can be stupid."

She laughed. "Truer words."

The bartender set the pitchers down on the bar. Kendall stacked the glasses into two towers while Pete grabbed the pitchers and they wove their way back to the table. When they stopped, he saw that the two open chairs were side by side, placing him sitting beside Kendall. Shit. He'd been hoping they'd be separated. It was hard enough being near her without having to sit beside her, feeling her leg against his and not being able to touch her. This was going to be agony.

He eased into the seat beside Gonzo, leaving Kendall the seat at the end of the table beside Ryan so she could talk with her brother.

Kendall's leg kept brushing against his. He didn't know if she was doing it on purpose or not, but it was driving him crazy.

"Here you go, Zip," Smitty said as he slid a beer down the table in front of Pete.

"Why do they call you Zip?" Theresa asked.

"Did you not see that snag he made in the fourth?" Gonzo asked.

"The snag?" Theresa looked blankly at them like Gonzo was speaking a different language.

"The diving catch," Kendall replied.

"Oh yeah, of course, but what does that have to do with the nickname?"

"Because he's lightning fast and zips all over the place," Smitty told her. His tone implied she wasn't too bright, which earned him a kick under the table from Pete. Smitty scowled back.

"Oh, that makes sense and is definitely a lot better than what I was thinking," Theresa said. She smirked at her friends as she picked up her margarita and took a sip.

"Okay, what was the look for? Why did you think we called him Zip?" Gonzo asked.

Theresa shrugged and took another sip of her drink. "I thought maybe he was really kinky."

"Kinky? Why the hell would we call him Zip?" Ryan asked.

"I don't know, like zip-ties, restraints, that kind of thing."

Kendall coughed, spurting her drink across the table. Pete bit back a smirk. It had been a resistance band, actually, but close enough.

Sam flicked a glance back and forth between Pete and Kendall. He withered slightly under the knowing stare of Kendall's good friend. "And here I thought maybe he had a lightning trigger in the bedroom."

Pete scowled at Kendall, then Sam, and growled, "No, I don't have a hair trigger in the bedroom. I'm fast where I need to be and slow when it counts."

He shot Kendall a sideways glance. When she wouldn't look at him, he stewed. What the hell had she told her friends? Sure, he'd been fast the first time, but he'd more than made up for it later.

"I don't know. I've always heard that pro-athletes are all talk and suck at the follow through."

"Well, I can't speak for these guys, but I can promise you this pro-athlete doesn't suck at anything," Smitty said as he leaned in closer to Sam and tucked her hair behind her ear making her giggle like a schoolgirl.

"All right, who wants to play pool?" Ryan asked.

"I'm game," Sam replied.

"Sure, I'll play," Smitty replied.

"Any other takers? We need a fourth." Ryan glanced around the table. The rest of the women didn't seem inclined to play. Pete knew he should, but the opportunity to spend time with Kendall without Ryan's prying eyes was too good to pass up.

"I'm in," Gonzo said as he pushed away from the table. He leaned down and whispered to Pete. "You owe me one, brother."

Pete winced. Guess he wasn't as subtle as he liked to think. Thank god Ryan seemed oblivious.

The moment the other men left, the women descended on him. "So, Pete, Kendall says she's known you since you were in high school," Theresa said.

"Uh yeah. Her brother and I billeted together when I first left home in the minors."

"And was she always as ridiculously gorgeous as she is now? Please tell me she went through an awkward phase," Jenna badgered.

Kendall narrowed her eyes as she mock glared at her friends and laughed. "Please don't answer that," she said to Pete.

He pictured Kendall as a teenager. She'd always been so shy around him. They'd barely talked when he was in high school. "I didn't know her that well, honestly."

Jenna leaned her elbows on the table and pinned him with a stare. "That didn't answer my question."

"Jenna," Kendall warned.

"What?" She blinked her eyes innocently. "I'm just curious what he thought of you when you were younger."

"Uh, yeah, she was always pretty, but she didn't talk much, so like I said, I didn't know her very well."

"Kendall not talk?" Jenna teased. "Are you sure we're talking about the same person?"

"Ha ha," Kendall mocked. "Very funny. I don't always talk."

"No, but I can't picture you being shy either," Jenna said.

Kendall shrugged. "I didn't come into my own until university."

"What was different about university?" Pete asked.

"I don't know. I guess I was finally out of Ryan's shadow and free to explore who I wanted to be."

"What do you mean?" he pressed.

"Oh, come on, you've been around my family. The sun shines out of Ryan's ass. He can do no wrong. It's kind of hard to leave your mark in his wake. University allowed me to test my light a little."

He studied her. Is that how she saw herself? Living in Ryan's shadow? He couldn't picture it. She seemed to shine on her own. She was so confident and sure of herself. In the time they'd spent together, he'd been amazed by how intelligent she was. She saw things in a way that he'd never seen before. It had been eye opening. Unfortunately, he liked who she'd become a little too much.

At the shyness on her face, he was unable to stop himself from reaching out to her. He cupped her knee with his hand and she looked over at him. He squeezed her leg. "I enjoyed getting to know you away from Ryan as well," he murmured quietly, so he thought only she would hear.

"Ahh, cute. So, what did you two get up to while Kendall stayed with you?" Jenna pressed.

"Jesus," Pete muttered. "Are your friends always like this?" he asked.

Kendall glared at Jenna. "No, they aren't. They are usually much better behaved."

"Sorry," Jenna replied. "I just want to make sure you appreciate how great our girl is."

"Jenna," Kendall growled.

"Okay, okay, I'll stop." Jenna held her hands out in surrender.

"Come on Jen, let's go watch them play pool," Theresa said as she stood up from the table. With drinks in hand, the two women wove their way towards the pool table, leaving Pete alone with Kendall.

He turned in his seat so he was facing Kendall. God, she was beautiful. "What exactly did you tell your friends about me? Between the kink, the speed and then the fourth degree there, clearly you mentioned we'd slept together."

She wrinkled her nose. "Sorry about that. Yeah, I told them what happened, but believe me, I didn't give them any indication you were quick."

He let his gaze trail slowly down her body, enjoying how she shivered beneath his stare. "Even when it was hard and fast I don't remember you complaining."

"Definitely no complaints." She leaned in closer and trailed her hand up his thigh. "Well, maybe one."

Shifting on his seat as her hand trailed closer to his junk, he flicked a glance towards the pool table, but no one was paying them any attention. "What complaint would that be?"

Her hand continued to trail up his thigh at a painstakingly slow pace. When she cupped him through his jeans, he bit back a groan. "That I can't do more than just this," she whispered and squeezed him tighter.

He glanced back at the group. Would anyone notice if they took off? Fuck, of course Ryan would notice if both Pete and Kendall were missing. Shit. He eyed the hallway to the washroom. Maybe?

When he looked back at Kendall, she sat watching him with an amused expression on her face. "What?" he asked.

"Just wondering if you figured out where you could take me?"

"Fuck. No, but the wheels are definitely spinning," he growled. "This is a bad fucking idea, though."

"Mmm-hmm," she murmured. "Does that mean you don't want to?"

"Christ no. I haven't been able to think about anything else since the moment I saw you sitting in the stands today." He picked up his beer and downed most of the contents.

"Me neither."

He picked up the edge of her shirt and rubbed it between his fingers. There was no way he could explain to her what it meant to him that she'd worn this today. "And seeing you in my jersey just kind of tipped the scales from wanting to needing to be with you."

"You need to be with me?" she asked.

As painful as it was to admit, he could give this to her. "More than I need my next breath."

"Good. I thought I was the only one feeling this way."

"Unfortunately not. You got any ideas?" Pete asked.

"I thought you pro-athletes were so good at the logistics of making sure you got laid after a game."

"Yeah, but I'm not usually trying to keep it a secret from my teammates. That kind of makes things a bit harder."

She chewed on her bottom lip, deep in thought, as she looked over at the pool table. "You could say you're tired and that you're going back to the hotel and then meet me at my place."

Pete stood up so fast the chair nearly toppled over and Kendall burst out laughing. "Easy, boy."

"Don't push me, Ken. I'm barely hanging on here."

"Good, I like you this way." She licked her lips, then stood up. She brushed her body against his as she stepped away from the table. She may as well have squeezed his cock. It would have had the same effect on him. His muscles tensed as he fought not to pull her against him.

It felt like he was walking a tightrope to keep his body in check. He didn't remember ever being this desperate to be with anyone. What had she done to him that he couldn't think about anything but her? Even today during the game, he'd been conscious of her every moment, and that was so unlike him. Normally, nothing distracted him from the game.

Going back to her place was a bad fucking idea, but there was no way he was missing out on this opportunity. "Text me your address," he growled before they walked towards their friends.

He stopped at the pool table. "I'm beat guys. I'm going to head back to the hotel and crash."

"Seriously, Grandpa? It's not even midnight," Smitty mocked.

"Some of us work harder than others out there," he replied. Puffing out his chest, he held his arms wide. "I mean, I did hit a grand slam. That takes a lot out of a guy." The only way to ensure these guys didn't ask too many questions was to start trash talking.

"Fuck you," Smitty replied.

"Ah, don't be jealous, man. Maybe you just need some clean living like me."

Smitty picked up his beer and took a long, healthy slug. "I'll pass. I'd rather hit a couple of ribbies and enjoy life than hit a dinger and need a nap."

Pete laughed. "Fair enough." He turned to Kendall's friends. "It was nice meeting you all."

"Nice meeting you too," they all sang in unison.

He looked at Kendall, then shrugged. What the hell, Ryan would expect him to hug her goodbye. He pulled her into a hug. "Nice seeing you, Ken," he said loud enough for everyone to hear, then whispered, "Be quick."

Stepping back, he flicked one last wave towards the group, then walked out of the bar. This night was turning out to be a lot better than he'd expected. Now he just had to wait for Kendall to tell him where she lived.

CHAPTER ELEVEN

Kendall glanced at her watch for the millionth time. How much longer before she could cut out without drawing suspicion?

"I have to go to the washroom," Sam announced as she linked arms with Kendall and pulled her away from the group towards the restroom. "What's going on? You've been acting weird."

"No, I haven't," Kendall protested.

"Uh, yeah, you have. What's up? Why did Pete leave so early?"

She grimaced. "He's waiting for me back at my place, and I'm just trying to figure out how to leave without my brother figuring out what's going on."

"Leave it to me." Sam pulled her into the washroom and leaned against the counter.

"I thought you had to go." Kendall pointed to the stall door.

"No, I just wanted to talk to you."

"Okay then." Kendall laughed.

"So, Pete is meeting you at your place? What happened to ending things and all that?"

"I probably should but—" She sighed. "He's just so damn sweet and sexy and god—"

"I get the appeal. He's very attractive." Sam pinned her with a look. "I just don't want you to get hurt."

"Me neither," Kendall admitted. "But I think I'm past the point of no return when it comes to him. No one else measures up." She faced the mirror and looked at herself. She couldn't hide from the truth. "He wants to meet, and I can't say no. Maybe I just need to let this burn out first and deal with whatever is left at the end."

"Just be careful, okay?" Sam said.

She turned, faced the mirror, and fluffed up her hair. Squaring her shoulders, Kendall made eye contact with her friend in the mirror. "I will. Thanks. Let's get back out there and make an excuse so I can get home."

When they walked back to their group, Jenna and Theresa were flirting mercilessly with the men. Kendall smiled, wondering if her friends would hook up with her brother's teammates this evening. It sucked that they could be so open about their attraction to each other, and she had to hide her attraction to Pete. Apparently, her friends weren't off limits, just she was.

"The drinks have hit me a little harder than normal tonight, so I think I need to cut out," Sam said.

"Oh, that's no good," Theresa groaned. "We just ordered another round."

"You should stay and finish them." Sam turned to Kendall. "I hate to do this, Ken, but I left my bag with my keys and stuff at your place so I can't get into my house."

"Oh no problem, I'll go with you."

"Are you sure? I hate to drag you home early."

"No, it's fine, don't worry about it," Kendall replied. She turned to her brother and hugged him. "It was great watching you today. I forgot how much fun it is to see you play."

"Thanks for coming. Any chance we can meet for lunch tomorrow before I have to head to warmup?" Ryan asked.

"Absolutely. Just text me in the morning and we'll figure out where and when to meet."

Kendall turned to the rest of the group. "Night all. Make good choices," she called.

Outside, she turned to Sam. "Thanks for doing this. Sorry you have to go home early."

"No problem. I wasn't hooking up with anyone anyway, so no big deal to go home early." Sam pulled up the Uber app. "It says they'll be ten minutes, so I'll just get picked up at your place, which should time out perfectly."

After dropping her phone in her purse, Sam raised her brow at Kendall. "What are you waiting for? Just cause I'm not hooking up doesn't mean you aren't. Let's go, girl."

When they rounded the corner towards Kendall's apartment, her heart pounded in her chest at the sight of Pete sitting with his back resting against the locked front door. When he saw them, he stood up. His gaze trailed slowly up her body like a caress.

"Damn," Sam whispered.

Kendall smacked her arm. "Shut up." She laughed.

Pete eyed Sam skeptically. "Don't worry, lover boy, my ride will be here any second," Sam taunted.

"I wasn't worried," Pete replied.

The Uber pulled up to the curb. Sam turned and gave Kendall a hug, then turned to Pete. "Treat her right," she ordered.

"Of course," he said.

As the car drove away, Pete stepped toward her. He threaded his hands into her hair and pulled her face to meet his. His lips brushed against hers. "Hi," he whispered against her mouth.

"Hi, I'm glad you're here," she said as her body melted into his.

"Fuck, me too," he groaned.

Kendall interlocked her hand through his. "Let's go upstairs." She pulled her keys out of her purse and unlocked the main door to let them into the building. At the elevator, Pete stood behind her and wrapped his arms around her waist. Neither of them spoke as they waited for the doors to open. Once inside the elevator, the doors closed. Kendall looked at their reflection in the mirror. "Are you sure this is a good idea?" she asked.

Pete turned her toward him and looked down at her face. The heated expression on his face sent the blood coursing through her veins. He backed her up against the wall and caged her in with his body. Resting his hands on the railing on either side of her, he stared down at her. "No, but I don't fucking care," he replied.

"Me neither," she whispered.

He leaned down and nuzzled his face against the curve of her neck. "What have you done to me, Ken? I can't stop thinking about you. The way you laugh, the way you smell." He ran his tongue up the length of her neck. "The way you taste."

She shivered at the feel of his hot, wet mouth against her neck. "I can't stop thinking about you either."

"Thank god." The elevator stopped and the doors slid open. Pete stepped back and threaded his fingers through hers.

Hand in hand, they walked down the hall to her place. Somehow, this felt different. It was like they were crossing a line tonight with this decision. It wasn't the desperate mating of their previous encounters.

Pete looked around her apartment. "I like it, it's very you."

"Thanks. Can I get you a drink or anything?" Why did she feel so nervous? This was Pete. It wasn't like they'd never done this before. She clasped her hands in front of herself and chewed her bottom lip.

"No, I'm good," he said. He stepped toward her and fingered the bottom edge of her jersey. "I'm going to have to give you more stuff with my name on it. Because holy shit."

She laughed at the look of open wonder on his face. "Oh yeah, it really works for you that much, huh?"

"Who knew?" he admitted.

"Guess you're kinkier than you thought," she teased.

"Certainly more fucking possessive than I'd ever imagined," he growled.

He wrapped the jersey around his fist and pulled, causing her to stumble toward him. He easily caught her body. His hands gripped her hips and he held her in place. She shivered at the sheer strength and power of his touch.

"You want to show me your bedroom?" he asked.

Unable to speak, she nodded. A slow, carnal smile spread across his face. "How come you seem nervous, Peanut?"

"I have no idea," she admitted.

His fingers tightened around her hips a moment before he hoisted her up. She squealed and wrapped her legs around his waist. "Why are you always picking me up?" she asked.

"I like feeling you in my arms and knowing you can't get away."

Her nipples beaded as lust coursed through her body. Damn, she shouldn't enjoy hearing him say that, but she really did. Not that she'd ever admit it to anyone.

"Last door on the right," she told him. She tightened her legs around his waist and held on as he walked down the hall to her room.

He paused at the edge of the bed and set her down on her feet. Dragging the back of his fingers across her cheek and gliding down her throat, his eyes narrowed as he watched the path of his hand. Pete's touch was feather light against her skin and she leaned into him, needing more. He slowly undid the first button on her jersey. Anticipation caused her nipples to tighten and she sucked in her bottom lip, eager for him to continue. His fingers again teased against her skin, driving her crazy as he moved to the next button. Her heart pounded in her chest as he pushed the edges of the shirt open, exposing her bra.

"God, you're beautiful," he said.

With the way he was looking at her, she believed it. No man had ever looked at her as reverently as Pete was looking at her now, as she stood before him clad in a shirt with his name on it. The feminist in her said she should be annoyed that he liked it so much. The woman in her fucking loved how powerful she felt to be needed this badly.

"I'm just going to leave this on for a little bit," he murmured as he undid the last button on the jersey.

"You are so weird," she laughed.

He shrugged, then trailed a finger along the curve of her breast, following the line of her demi-cut bra. He flicked open the front closure, exposing her breasts. Cupping them in his hands, he bent his head and swiped his tongue against one nipple.

She closed her eyes and dropped her head back as heat pooled in her core from the contact. He undid her jeans and pushed them down her legs till they puddled at her feet. She swayed, thankful for the mattress pressing against the backs of her knees. She sat down, leaned back, and rested on her elbows as she looked at him.

Pete kneeled down between her legs and pulled her jeans off and chucked them behind him. He grabbed her ankle and placed it on his shoulder. Gliding his palm up her calf, she shifted her hips in anticipation. *Oh god, yes please.* Unable to take her eyes off him, she wiggled closer. When Pete ran his tongue up her inner thigh, she moaned.

"Lie down," he ordered.

The first swipe of his tongue along her slit made her back bow off the mattress. "Yes," she hissed.

He swirled his tongue around her clit, then inserted first one finger, then a second inside her. *Fuck.* She threaded her hands through his brown hair to hold his head where she wanted him, and he chuckled against her. The vibration of his laughter and his hot breath made her pussy clench with need, and she wrapped her legs around his neck. He sucked her clit into his mouth. Her eyes dropped closed and she hissed out a breath as she let the sensation flow through her. Widening her legs, she pressed into him. He dragged his teeth against the tight bud, making her squirm. My god, the man knew his way around her body.

Her muscles pulled up tight and she sucked in air as her orgasm built. Pete curled his fingers inside her and rubbed against that spot that previously only her toys could hit. "Don't stop, don't stop," she begged.

Pete chuckled before he nipped her clit between his teeth. She grabbed his head with both hands, holding him in place. Her legs clamped tightly around his ears of their own volition as she screamed out her release. His tongue kept swirling and flicking against her clit, and the sensation built again. It was too much. There was no way. She gasped for breath and tried to push his head away, but he held her tight. "Not yet." His gravelly voice vibrated against her core.

"Seriously, Pete, I can't," she begged.

"I think you can," he commanded. He drew hard on her clit and pressed his fingers firmly against her g-spot. Her whole body pulled tight as she arched off the bed. The orgasm ripped through with a tsunami force, making her collapse against the bed as she gasped for breath.

Finally, she popped her eyes open and looked down her body where Pete sat resting on his knees between her legs with a satisfied, purely male look on his face. "Well, I hope you're pleased with yourself, because I think you killed me. My body can't move, so you're out of luck," Kendall told him.

Pete grinned. "I'm pretty sure you can rally." He pressed a kiss to the inside of her knee, then stood up. He reached behind his head and peeled his shirt off one handed and tossed it towards her pants.

Her eyes lingered on the v-cut of his hip bones and a fresh wave of lust coursed through her body. Okay, he was right, she could definitely rally. She pushed herself up on her elbows so she could watch him finish undressing.

A smirk crossed Pete's face. "Got a second wind?"

"Something like that."

Grabbing a condom out of his pocket, he held it between his fingers as he looked at her. He pushed his jeans and boxers down in one fell swoop. His long, thick cock jutted straight out from his body and she swallowed past the lump in her throat. God, this man affected her.

With the condom in place, he stepped toward the bed. "On your knees, Ken," he demanded.

Pushing herself up on her knees, she slid down to the edge of the mattress. Pete's firm hands gripped her hips and he pulled her into place. She gasped at the raw power of his touch. His body trembled against her, like he was hanging on by a thread.

He pressed himself against her core and paused, as if waiting for her to give the okay. She pushed back against him. The movement, all the permission he needed. He gripped her hips as he drove forward, making them both moan. He thrust into her hard and fast. His arm wrapped around her waist, and he shifted her hips to a higher angle where he wanted her. He drove deep and she gasped at how full she felt. Kendall's knees barely rested on the bed as Pete held her in place with sheer strength. He shifted them again and her knees fully popped off the bed. The only thing holding her up were her hands and Pete's strength. "Oh," she gasped.

"Hold on," he growled.

Kendall moved to her elbows and dropped her head forward as Pete drove into her. His fingers dug into her hips as he grunted behind her. "This okay?"

Was he kidding? This was unfreaking believable. She'd never been fucked so deeply in her life. She hadn't known it was possible to feel like this. "Don't stop," she demanded.

"I don't plan to."

Her fingers curled into the blankets as she tried to hold herself in place. Their bodies slapped together. The raw, animal sound pulsed through the room. Her muscles clenched tightly as another orgasm built inside her. Pete shifted ever so slightly, and the orgasm tore through her body, pulling all her muscles tight. She tried not to collapse on the mattress as what little strength she had left gave out. His grip tightened to hold her in place as he grunted out his own orgasm.

Pete eased her back onto the bed and stepped back. She was done. Kendall couldn't even lift her head.

"Now, are you really dead?" Pete teased.

"Ugh." The unintelligible sound that she forced out of her mouth made Pete laugh.

He slapped her on the ass and she didn't even have the energy to squeal or shift. A moment later, she felt him return. He dragged her up higher onto the mattress, so their heads were on the pillow and he pulled her against his body with his front resting against her back.

God, now he was spooning her. Could this night get any better? That was the last thought she had before she drifted off to sleep.

Something pulled her out of her sleep. The room was dark, and she felt Pete's body shifting behind her.

"I should get going," he whispered against her neck.

"Already?" she complained.

"It's five o'clock in the morning. If I don't go now, I'll be liable to run into some of the guys, and I don't need to explain this."

"How would you explain it?"

"I don't have a clue." He pulled her tightly against his body. His breath was hot against the curve of her neck as they lay spooned together.

"I wish this was different," she said.

"Yeah, I just don't know how it could be."

And therein lay the problem. There could be no future with him living in San Diego and her here. Was there a way they could make this work? If there was, she didn't have the first flipping clue how to make that happen when he was terrified of Ryan finding out.

"Me neither," she whispered.

He pulled on her hip, forcing her to roll over and face him. She wrapped her arms around his neck and threw her leg over his hip so they were pressed completely against each other. They lay in silence for several minutes before Pete finally sighed. "I gotta go. Thanks for last night. I know this made it harder, but I don't regret it."

"I have no regrets. Sadly, I'll take what I can get." She closed her eyes and rested her forehead against his. She probably shouldn't have admitted that out loud.

He pressed a kiss to her lips. "Bye." He slid out of bed.

She should probably be a good hostess and walk him to the door, but she just didn't have the energy. All she wanted to do was curl up and cry. She'd finally found a person she truly wanted to be with. Someone she could picture a life with and they couldn't be together. How was that fair?

CHAPTER TWELVE

Wednesday night back at his place, Pete lay back on his bed and stared up at the ceiling. What the hell was the matter with him? Thoughts of Kendall filled his brain. She'd only been here a week with him before he went off to training camp. His place shouldn't feel so empty after such a short period of time.

He grabbed the baseball from the bedside drawer and threw it up in the air and caught it. The easy game of catch had always helped him think. He could clear away the crap and just zone out and let his brain do what it needed to do to process.

Unfortunately, the longer he tossed the ball the more his brain kept going back to how empty his place felt without Kendall. Fuck. He was the king of casual. Their week-long hookup should have been perfect, so why could he not stop thinking about her? He never should have hooked up with her again in Atlanta. It made him want things he couldn't have. Relationships didn't last, it was just prolonging the inevitable.

His phone buzzed on the bedside table beside him. He saw his buddy Jaxon's name on the screen before he swiped to pick it up.

"Hey Jax, what's up?"

"Sorry, I should probably do the polite conversation thing first, but fuck it. Lia's pregnant."

"Holy shit, you're going to be a dad?" A smile split across Pete's face as he pictured his oldest friend with a baby. "That's amazing. Congrats."

"Thanks. We aren't telling most people for a couple months still, but Li agreed we could tell you. I was driving her crazy and had to tell somebody."

"How's she feeling?"

"Nauseous, but I guess that's to be expected," Jaxon replied.

Pete heard feet scuffling in the background and he smiled. Typical Jaxon, he always paced when he was anxious or excited. He'd practically worn holes in the carpet in his bedroom as a kid. Jax's mom kept buying carpet runners for his room because she didn't like what he was doing to her floors.

"Relax man, and breathe," Pete said.

Jaxon exhaled deeply. "I know. There's just a lot to learn and a lot to plan for."

"That's why you have nine months to do it. You've got lots of time."

"Don't laugh at me, asshole. This is...fuck... fucking incredible. I can't even—"

"You and Lia are going to be amazing parents." What a difference a year could make. This time last year, Lia and Jaxon had been on the verge of separation and now they were having a baby. Honestly, it kind of shocked him they'd been able to turn things around. Definitely not the norm, judging by divorce rates. Most people he knew would have given up when things got that hard, but they'd come through it all stronger than ever. And now they were having a baby. Holy shit.

"How'd you know Lia was the one?" Pete asked.

"Whoa, where'd that come from? Have you met someone?"

"No, maybe, I don't know. Fuck." He sighed. "She's definitely got me in knots."

"Lia, Pete's in love," Jaxon yelled.

"What? Don't tell her that. I'm not in love. I'm just in..."

Lia's voice broke into the conversation. "Put him on speakerphone."

"Jax, don't—" Pete had barely started to speak when Lia's voice chirped in. "So, tell me about this girl that has you all tangled up in knots," Lia said.

"She doesn't have me tangled up," he grumbled.

Lia's laughter tinkled across the line. "Clearly."

"She's just different. It was supposed to be a quick fling, but I don't know, it's complicated."

"It's always complicated, my man," Jax replied. "But if a woman finally has you wondering about more, then you should see where that might go."

"It can't go anywhere. That's the problem." Maybe that's all this was. His reaction to being told no. Ever since he was a kid when someone told him he couldn't have something, he wanted it. And he did everything in his power to get it. Hell, he was a trailer park kid who'd made it to the major leagues, he'd had nothing but no's growing up.

"Why can't it go anywhere? She's not married, is she?" Jaxon growled.

"Fuck, no, Jesus, you know I would never do that." He tossed the ball up in the air and caught it again. "She doesn't live here and she's a friend's sister, so it's all sorts of messed up."

"But you like her?" Lia asked.

He thought back to seeing her in Atlanta, then how it had been when she'd stayed with him. How waking up with her every morning and seeing her in his kitchen felt. He'd never had that with any woman before. Normally, he just wanted them to get the hell out of there. God forbid they touch his stuff and yet he'd let Kendall rearrange his pantry because she didn't think it made sense the way it was. He had to admit her way was better.

"Yeah, I like her," he agreed. "But she doesn't live here and if her brother found out..." He shuddered. His friendship with Ryan would be over.

"Why did you start something with her if you were worried about her brother?" Lia asked.

"Let's just say she should have been a lawyer and was very convincing about the benefits of a temporary fling." He grinned. The pros and cons list was still stuck to the board in the gym where Kendall had placed it.

"Does she want more?" Lia asked.

"She was definitely open to us continuing to talk."

"This is the first time I've actually heard you talk about something more with a woman. I never thought I'd see the day. I think it's worth continuing to talk to her at least," Jax said. "Hell, during the season, you never want to date anyway, so chatting with someone in a different town is probably good. Who knows, maybe you'll realize it was just hot sex and not something real and you won't have to worry about it anymore."

"Yeah, maybe," Pete mumbled. Except it didn't feel like it was just about the sex with Kendall. But what the hell did he know about having a relationship? His longest one had been two weeks. It never felt worth it to put in the effort. Relationships didn't last anyway. And the ones that did, often shouldn't.

"You're already in it this far, why not see where it goes?" Jax pressed.

"Thanks. And sorry I hijacked your phone call to deal with my shit. I'm so happy for you both. I can't wait to be an uncle." He couldn't imagine himself ever being in a relationship with someone and wanting to have kids with them. Sure, the idea of kids was nice in theory, but there was no way he would put a kid through what he'd experienced growing up.

"Thanks," Lia replied.

"Now stop chucking your little ball around and call the girl," Jax said.

"Fuck you." He laughed and hung up the phone.

Were they right? Should he call her? He spun his phone around in his hand. What was the harm in continuing to talk to Kendall? It wasn't like this could go anywhere with her living on the other side of the country. But there was no harm in talking.

Mooch glided into the bedroom and crawled under the bed. A moment later, he crawled back out, dragging a piece of fabric. He leaned over and scooped up

Kendall's scarf from the floor. Guess that answered that question. Now he had to call her.

He snapped a picture of the scarf and hit send. Waited a minute and dialed her number.

"Look what Mooch found under my bed," he said when she picked up the phone.

"Maybe I left it there on purpose, so you'd be forced to call me." Her teasing tone went directly to his cock. Damn, this woman affected him.

"Did you?"

"No, it never occurred to me something like that would work with you, otherwise I might have."

"Clearly it would have worked." He leaned back on the bed and placed his arm behind his head to settle in to chat with her.

"I thought we decided it wasn't a good idea to try to drag this thing out," she said.

"Well, hear me out. It would drag things out if we tried to see each other and travel back and forth and all that crap. But there's nothing wrong with us being friends and talking."

"Friends?" Her voice hitched up in question, like she didn't believe him.

"Well, you know, maybe friends who have phone sex."

"I don't have phone sex with my friends, Pete." He could practically hear the smirk in her voice.

"Friends with benefits. Although I mean—it's phone sex, that's like having an imaginary friend, so it hardly even counts as crossing that line."

Kendall laughed. "An imaginary friend, huh? Okay, is that what we're calling it now?"

Pleased with himself for coming up with the idea, he leaned back and tucked his hand behind his head. "Yep, that's why it's perfect that we keep talking. Everyone needs a friend they can be themselves with and get a little dirty."

"Oh really, and you have these kinds of friends?"

"No, but I totally should. Come on, help a guy out. You wouldn't want me to miss out on this life experience, would you? This is bucket list shit. What kind of friend would you be if you didn't help me out?"

Kendall snorted. "You're an idiot."

"Yeah, but you're intrigued, right?" He shifted on the bed and widened his legs as his cock twitched as he listened to her husky laugh.

"Well, I'd hate to deprive the great Pete Saunders of a life goal."

"I know. It's sad and I'm ashamed to admit it, but I've never had proper phone sex. I would be mocked mercilessly and laughed out of the changing room if the guys knew that."

"Oh god forbid." She laughed. "But I thought you didn't want the guys on the team to know about us."

He shifted uncomfortably. "I don't, but they don't need to know where I gained this experience, do they?"

"I don't want to be your dirty secret, Pete," she whispered.

"It's not like that, Ken."

"Then what would it be like?" she asked.

He sat up and ran his fingers through his hair. What the hell was he asking of her, exactly? "I don't know." He sighed. "I just know I'd like to keep talking to you, but I don't know what that means." He looked down at the scarf on his bed and ran it through his fingers. "I'm sorry. I know that's not fair to you."

"No, it's not, but I'm not ready for whatever this is to be done either," she admitted.

"Are we going to do this phone friends with bennies thing?" he asked.

"But are we friends, Pete?"

Pete shrugged. "I don't know. I mean, I think we're friends."

"Just friends?" she asked.

He sighed. "What else can we be? You live there, I live in San Diego. You're Ry's sister, he'd fucking kill me if he knew I'd even thought about touching you, let alone what we have done." He paused as he tried to think of how to articulate what he wanted to say. "I'm not a good bet, Ken. I'm the guy you have fun with while you wait for Mr. Right. I'm someone to kill time with. I mean you're dating, right?"

"Sort of. I'm definitely not dating often."

"Okay, you keep dating and we chat on the side, maybe have a little phone sex to take the edge off while you look for your dream guy."

"And what do you get out of this while I'm looking for Mr. Right?"

"Um, did you miss the part about the phone sex?"

"I'm being serious, Pete."

"Look, I know this doesn't make a hell of a lot of sense. All I know is I thought about you the whole time I was at camp. I kept picking up the phone to call you or text you and couldn't because we put this stupid rule in place." He sighed. "And then seeing you in Atlanta...well we both know how that went."

"Yeah, I've thought about you a lot, too."

"What are you saying?" he asked.

"I'm saying I'm fine with us continuing to talk. I'd like that. But I want you to be open to seeing if this could go somewhere."

"But where can it go?"

"I don't know. I mean jobs change, right? You could get transferred to a different team. I could ask for a transfer. Stuff changes all the time."

"I'm not going anywhere. I just signed a five-year deal."

"Okay, but all I'm saying is if we are going to talk you can't completely write this off as nothing."

"But this isn't exclusive right, you're going to keep dating and trying to meet someone. Because I'm serious Kendall, I'm not that guy. As much as I want to keep doing whatever this is, I don't want to hurt you and I will if you go into this thinking this is going to have a white picket fence kind of ending. That's not who I am."

"I know exactly who you are, Pete," she replied.

What did that mean, exactly? God, how lame was it that he wanted to ask her how she saw him? "Are we doing this?" He held his breath as he waited for her answer.

"Yeah, we're doing this."

He breathed a sigh of relief. "Thank fuck." The knot in his stomach eased. This was possibly the dumbest idea he'd ever had, but the idea of not talking to Kendall didn't sit well with him. She'd probably meet some brilliant doctor or lawyer who wanted to have a couple of kids and a house in the suburbs, and she'd be done with him, but until then. Why couldn't they have a friendship on the side? It was just some conversation and hopefully some phone sex, which, like he'd said, didn't really count. He pictured Kendall masturbating, and his cock throbbed against his pants. Okay, maybe it kind of counted.

"You do realize this means touching yourself and not actual sex, right?" she joked.

"Semantics," he said, as a smile split across his face. "So, we're going to be phone sex buddies?"

Kendall laughed. "Well, hopefully we'll be doing more than just having phone sex."

"Facetime sex?" he asked. He could definitely get on board with watching Kendall masturbate while she talked to him.

"I meant maybe we could also talk like friends as well, you perv."

"Yeah, yeah, that too," he teased. Holding her scarf in his hand, he lay back down on the bed. Now that he had that image in his mind, he couldn't think of anything else. "Hang up, Kendall, and I'm calling you back on Facetime, so I can see you."

"Okay," she whispered.

Two weeks later, Kendall leaned against the elevator wall as she waited for it to ascend to her floor. Tonight had been a complete bust. What had she been thinking, letting her friends convince her to go on a date?

Jenna had been trying to get her to go out with her coworker since before she went to San Diego, but she'd never gone. When the girls heard about her arrangement with Pete, they'd badgered her even more to go on the date. If what she had with Pete was supposed to be casual, then she needed to get out there, otherwise it wasn't casual. And they were right.

The problem was she'd always compared men to Pete and now that she knew what he was like intimately, it was even harder not to compare. And no one was Pete Saunders. It didn't bode well.

Her phone buzzed and she dug into her purse as she walked down the hallway to her apartment.

Speak of the devil. "Hey Pete,"

"Hey. How was your day?"

She held her phone between her ear and shoulder as she put the keys in the lock and opened her door. "Long. How was yours?"

"Are you just getting home now?" he asked.

She sighed. Should she tell him? He'd said he thought she would try to meet someone. Not to pin any hopes on him and something happening between them. "I was on a date."

"What? You went on a date tonight?"

Hope sprang in her chest. He wouldn't be jealous if didn't care about her. "Yeah. Why do you sound like that? I thought we agreed we were just friends and were going to date other people."

"We are. I was just surprised you went out tonight. I mean, it's a work night."

"Right, grandpa. It's 10 o'clock and I'm home."

"Are you still dressed from your date?"

"Yeah, I just walked in the door when you called."

"K, hang up, I'm Facetiming you," he said and hung up.

She looked down at her phone when he hung up. What the hell?

Her phone rang and she answered the video call.

"Damn," Pete murmured. "You got all dressed up for your date."

"Well, it was a date."

"Let me see your outfit," he demanded.

"Why?"

"I don't know, because I want to see what you wore on your date."

"Why, Pete?"

"I don't fucking know," he growled.

"I think you do," she whispered. A sliver of hope spread through her chest at the possessive note in his voice. The fact that he didn't sound happy about her dating had to be a good sign, right?

"Because I'm jealous all right." He ran his hand through his hair. "I don't have any right to be. I know we're just friends but... just show me what you wore okay?"

She tilted her phone so he could see her outfit.

"Jesus, you look fucking hot," he groaned. "How was the date, or do I want to know?"

"Well, I'm home by 10 o'clock so you tell me."

"That good, huh?" A cocky smile curled up the corner of his mouth.

"That good." She wrinkled her nose. "He called me baby."

"What's wrong with that? You like when I call you baby."

"There's a difference between you calling me baby during sex and some dude calling me baby on a first date." She cringed as she thought about it. "The way he said it, I kept expecting him to say call me daddy."

Pete snorted. "Nice. So uh... big daddy wasn't the guy for you, huh?"

"No, definitely not."

"Well then, I guess it's a good thing you have me around to help fill the time while you wait for the dream guy to show up."

She tilted the phone away so he didn't see her face. Unfortunately, she was afraid she'd already met her dream guy. He just didn't want the position.

"Where'd you go?" Pete asked.

She tilted the phone back to her face. "Sorry, I'm here."

"Other than the date, how was your day?"

"It was good, long. I'm still dealing with a ton of issues in the San Diego office. I don't know why they don't just replace that asshat Mark. I fielded three calls from staff there and then had to talk to the clients to smooth things over. He's a freakin' nightmare." She dropped down onto the couch. "It would be fine if he was willing to take constructive criticism but he's not. He just becomes a defensive dick." She rolled her neck to ease the tension that had been lingering all day.

"I'm sorry, babe. I wish I was there to rub your neck. You look like you have a headache brewing."

"I do." She opened her eyes and looked at him on the screen. The worry on his face warmed her chest. Pete might not think he was boyfriend material, but he was.

"So how did your game go tonight?" she asked.

"Not great, we lost 4-2."

"How'd you play?"

He shifted his body and Mooch came into view. "Are you snuggling your cat?"

"No, he's sitting with me. We aren't snuggling," he grumbled.

"Keep telling yourself that, buddy. I'm looking right at you and you're totally snuggling." Just as she spoke, the cat let out a loud purr that made them both laugh.

"Dude, not cool." Pete shook his head as he looked down at the cat. "How am I going to convince her I'm a tough guy if you go and purr and give it all away?"

"Hate to break it to you, but that ship has sailed. Mooch made that fact known long ago." She kicked off her heels and went into the kitchen to pour herself a glass of water.

Taking her glass with her, she wandered down the hallway to her bedroom. "How'd you play?" she asked again as she propped her pillows up against the bed-frame and sat down.

"Personally, I played fine. It wasn't our best showing on the sticks, but other than that, not bad. We were holding our own until the last inning when Sanchez hit a two-run double for the win."

"He's not San Fran's cleanup hitter for nothing," she replied.

Pete's smile lit up the screen. "The fact that you know that is so freaking hot."

Kendall rolled her eyes. "Me knowing baseball players is hot?"

"So hot."

The desire in Pete's voice made her nipples pull tightly against her bra, and she smiled at him through the screen.

Pete shifted on the couch and pushed Mooch off his lap. "You know, they say having an orgasm is one of the best things for a headache."

"Oh yeah, who's this elusive 'they'?" Kendall asked. She knew where this conversation was heading. If she was smart, she'd make him suffer and go without. He was the one who was encouraging her to date other people. It would serve him right if she denied him. But dammit, she wanted him just as badly as he seemed to want her.

"It's in all the medical books. Hell, Google it. It's probably the first headache remedy that comes up."

Kendall snorted at the air of confidence in which Pete spoke about the power of orgasms. "Does this line usually work for you?" she asked.

"Don't know. I've never tried it before." He quirked an eyebrow at her. "How's it working?"

If she was honest, the jealousy thing was working a hell of a lot better, but there was no way she was admitting that.

"Eh, not your best work," she teased.

"Damn, Atlanta has made you cold, Ken. You were so sweet when you were here. I'm not used to this side of you."

Kendall snickered. "You're such a goof."

"It's part of my charm." Their eyes connected through the screen and Kendall sighed. She wished she could see him in person. Facetime was great, but it didn't compare to feeling someone near you.

"Why don't you go run yourself a bath, and I'll keep you company while you relax."

"You just want to see me naked."

Pete clasped his hand to his heart. "Ouch, this is purely altruistic, I'll have you know. I mean, if you get inspired to test the theory on headache relief while you're having a soak, who am I to stand in your way?"

She had to admit, a nice bath did sound lovely. Today had been a bit of a bitch. She pushed off the bed and strolled into the bathroom. "Don't get your hopes up, mister," she warned.

"I wouldn't dream of it." Pete shoved off the couch. "I think I'll join you."

The tub filled with water and she poured in lavender bubble bath for her headache.

"Ah, you get bubbles?" Pete complained. "That's not fair."

"Sorry, buddy, you gotta buy your own." Kendall picked up a handful of bubbles and blew them, sending them floating through the air.

With the tub filled, she peeled off her clothes and eased herself into the water. The hot water glided over her skin and she moaned. God, that felt good.

"Jesus, you and those freaking sex noises you make," Pete growled.

"I didn't make a sex noise, and I defy anyone not to moan when they get into a hot bath."

"Sure," Pete snickered.

Moments later, she heard Pete moan as he slid into his own bath. "Okay, maybe you were right," Pete admitted.

Kendall dropped her head back against her bath pillow and closed her eyes. With her phone resting on the shelf beside the tub, she couldn't see Pete, but she could hear him shifting in the water. Somehow, this felt more intimate than anything they had done before. Why? She couldn't say.

She trailed her hand down her stomach, wishing it was Pete's hand. Even in the hot water, goosebumps broke out on her skin and she shivered.

"Are you touching yourself, Ken?"

"Maybe," she taunted.

"Jesus, please tell me you are." Pete must have shifted as the sound of water sloshing cut through the air.

"Mmm, this would feel better if it was your hand," she murmured.

"Pretend it is," he ordered. "I'm tracing my hand over the curve of your breast."

Kendall shifted her hand back up her body, following Pete's direction.

"Gently swirl your finger around your nipple, Ken."

She teased her nipple and it puckered beneath her touch. She slipped her hand over to her other breast and did the same to that nipple.

"Glide your hand down your stomach, caressing your belly, and slowly creep down. Your fingers are just brushing against the top of your mound. The hair moving in the water swirls against your fingers." He paused. "Wait. Don't move, anticipate. Can you picture me watching you, Ken?"

"Yes," she moaned. God, why was he so good at this? She squirmed against the tub, dying to move her hand lower.

"Pinch your nipple with your other hand." His husky voice glided over her like a caress. She did what she was told and her head dropped back. She closed her eyes, pretending it was Pete's hand, Pete's breath on her rather than the cool breeze of the bathroom fan.

"Touch yourself, Ken. Tell me what you feel like."

"Hot, wet, needy."

"Jesus," Pete groaned. "Put your finger inside yourself."

She moaned as she inserted her finger.

"Good girl." She heard water sloshing again and she could picture Pete stroking his cock as he directed her to touch herself. Her pussy clenched around her finger, and she moaned again.

"Rub your clit, pretend it's my tongue."

Kendall rubbed her clit softly at first, then harder as the orgasm built.

"That's it, Ken," Pete growled. "Make yourself come."

She pinched her clit hard and she screamed out her release. Pete's grunts filled the room as he came right behind her.

Kendall dropped her head against the bath pillow as she tried to catch her breath. Holy shit, that was intense. Normally, when they did that, they both had the phone angled so they could see each other. This time it was more like phone sex, where neither of them could see the other. It was just up to what she could hear and what she could imagine. Both ways were freaking hot.

"Wow." Pete's voice brought her back to the present.

"No kidding."

"How's the headache?"

Kendall opened her eyes and rolled her neck. The headache was much better. "Nobody likes a braggart, Peter."

His chuckle glided across her skin, wrapping around her with its warmth. "I'm not saying a word. But I'm glad you're feeling better."

Kendall pulled the drain from the tub and pushed herself to stand. She wrapped a towel around her body and picked up her phone so she could see Pete. She smiled when she saw his face appear on the screen. His cheeks flushed from the heat of the bath and his orgasm. He shoved his damp hair off his forehead as he looked at her.

"Meet you in bed?" he asked.

"Sounds good." Kendall set the phone down on the edge of the bedside table. She stepped into her pajamas, then crawled beneath the sheets. Positioned in bed, she picked her phone back up and waited for Pete to join her.

She could hear Pete shuffling around as he got ready for bed. Moments later, she caught a glimpse of him as he came back on screen. He covered a huge yawn with his palm.

"I should let you go, you're clearly exhausted."

"Sorry," he admitted.

"Don't be. You guys are off to Cincinnati next?"

"Yeah, we leave for the airport at 6 tomorrow morning."

"Okay, I'm going to let you go so you can get some sleep. Good luck against Cincy."

"Thanks." Pete paused and pursed his lips like he wasn't sure if he should say something."

"What?" she pressed.

"Selfishly, I'm glad your date sucked. I know I shouldn't say that, but it's true." He exhaled audibly. "I was feeling kind of shitty about the loss tonight, and I'm glad I got to see you before I went to bed."

"I'm glad my date sucked, too. Night Pete."

"Night Ken. Sweet dreams."

She flicked the button to disconnect the call. Kendall held her phone against her chest and sighed. Chatting with Pete at the end of the night even for five minutes was so much better than a shitty in person date with an asshole.

She glanced down at the phone in her hand. Pete calling tonight because he knew she'd make him feel better had to be a good sign. His jealousy about her date certainly was. She did a little butt wiggle dance on her bed. He was starting to come around.

CHAPTER THIRTEEN

Kendall gazed down at her phone and the picture of Pete's bare chest she had made as her background. Her eyes lingered on the V-cut of his hipbones. Damn, there was something to be said for a professional athlete's body. It was very clear he spent hours in the gym to get that physique and lord, was it worth the time spent.

A knock sounded at her office door and she snapped her eyes off her phone. *Shit.*

"Sandra, hi, what can I do for you?" she asked her boss. Perfect. Her boss had just caught her ogling a semi-naked photo on her phone when she was supposed to be working.

Sandra dropped into the chair opposite Kendall's desk. "We are having some more difficulties with the San Diego office."

"Okay." She grabbed a pad of paper off the corner of her desk to take notes. "The same issues as before?"

"Yes. We were really impressed with what you were able to accomplish in the two weeks while you were there and what you've continued to do for them since you've been back. In two months, you've been able to do more for the San Diego office than we've been able to do in the last year."

"I'm glad." Kendall smiled at her boss. Where was she going with this?

"On that note. How would you feel about a transfer?"

"What?" Kendall sat up straight in her chair. They wanted to move her to San Diego?

"Before you say anything. I want you to know this would be a promotion. We'd like you to consider taking over as manager of the San Diego branch. As you know, the interim manager we put in place when we fired Mark didn't work out. The staff there were all impressed with you and we've had several requests from their office to have you back."

"But moving to San Diego, that's a big change," Kendall murmured. Her brain was firing in a million different directions. She loved her job and life in Atlanta. But her brother and Pete were in San Diego. In San Diego, she could be in charge of the team rather than just a cog in the wheel. It was an opportunity she may never get if she stayed in Atlanta.

"We know it's a lot to ask. It would be a forty percent pay increase, plus moving expenses." Sandra leaned forward in her chair. "I truly believe with you at the helm in San Diego the firm could really flourish. I recognize your talents are not being fully utilized here. In San Diego you could soar."

"I'm flattered. This is a lot to process." Needing to do something with her hands, she picked up her water bottle and took a sip. "I'm not saying no, but can I take a few days to think about it?"

"Of course. What I'd like to do is to have you go back there next week. But go in with an eye to running the place rather than going in to fix a few problems. I think if you take a couple weeks working there it will help you get a feel for whether you want the job or not. If you decide it isn't the right fit for you, then no hard feelings, things will stay the same. But if you decide you want it, then we'd like to make the move as soon as possible so you can start putting your mark on the place."

Either way, she'd be back in San Diego next week. She could see Pete in person and figure out just where the hell things stood between them.

"I will definitely consider it, and I'd be happy to go to San Diego next week and take a look at things." She stood up and shook her boss's hand. "I'm honored to have been considered for this position."

"You aren't being considered Kendall. You're who we want. No one could do a better job than you. Of that I'm sure."

"Thank you," she replied.

Sandra walked out of the room and Kendall dropped down into her seat. *Holy shit.*

She shimmied in her chair in a little celebratory dance. Whether or not she took the job, she felt like that Sally Field Oscar meme. *You like me, you really like me.* They wanted her to run the entire San Diego office. *Oh, my god. This was amazing.* She sat staring out her office window for several minutes as she processed the information. What would moving look like? Did she want the job? It was significantly more responsibility. She'd be living in the same city as Pete, not just visiting. Would he want to pursue something with her?

Grabbing her phone, she pulled up Pete's name. The phone rang several times before he finally picked up.

"Hey, what are you doing calling me in the middle of the day?" he asked.

"My boss just left. They need me back in San Diego next week."

"Really?"

"Yep. So I was thinking we could maybe have some in-person sex rather than doing the Facetime thing while I was there."

"Would you be able to swing that since Ryan's in town and there's no way he's not making you stay with him?"

"Yeah, but he doesn't need to know my work schedule. I could have late meetings, or maybe I'll just stay in a hotel this time."

Pete made a strange sound. "Yeah, there's no way you can get away with staying in a hotel when he's home after you stayed with me last time."

She wrinkled her nose. "True, but like I said, I could have work dinners and meetings. We could figure something out if you wanted." Why did he seem so hesitant? "Do you not want to see me?"

"What? No, it's not that at all. I'm just trying to figure out the logistics of seeing you with Ryan around."

"It won't be that bad, trust me." She looked at the calendar on her desk. "What if I fly in Friday and tell Ryan I'm coming in on Sunday night? That would give us most of the weekend together, and then we can play the rest of the week by ear."

Pete cleared his throat. "I don't want you to have to lie to your brother."

"Oh my god, Pete, seriously, get over it. I am a grown ass woman. If I want to spend the weekend with you, I will. The only reason I would fudge things with my brother is to keep you happy. I couldn't care less if he knows where I am."

He coughed. "He definitely can't know where you are." Silence hung on the line as she waited for him to speak again. "Are you sure this is a good idea, Ken? I mean..."

"Do you want to see me?" she asked.

"Yeah," he groaned.

"Perfect, then. I'll fly in Friday and go to Ryan's on Sunday. End of discussion."

"Okay. You're a bad influence on me, you know," he complained, making her laugh. No one had ever said she was a bad influence before. She was a rule follower. A good girl. She smiled to herself. She kind of liked the idea that Pete found her so enticing he was willing to break a few rules to be with her.

"I'll make it worth your while, baby," she said suggestively.

"Of that, I have no doubt. That's the problem. I'm kind of blindly following you to hell," he muttered.

"But what a way to go," she teased.

"No fucking kidding."

"It'll be fine Pete, don't worry so much. Ryan will be none the wiser and we can enjoy some face-to-face time, which I think we both really want."

"Unfortunately, there's nothing I'd like more than to see you in person."

"Why's that unfortunate? It seems like a good thing."

"Because I shouldn't want you this much." He sighed. "You can do so much better than a guy like me."

"I like how much you want me." Her stomach fluttered at the heat in his voice. She'd never felt so desirable in her life. The way Pete looked at her, the way he made her body feel. It was intoxicating. She was going to do everything she could to convince him that what they had was worth holding onto. Despite what her brother might think.

"I better get back to work. I'll talk to you later," she said and hung up the phone.

Kendall eyed the clock on the dashboard and bit back a groan. She'd caught the earliest direct flight she could, but with delays and traffic to Pete's place, it was already 12:30 and he had to be at the stadium before 3:00. At this rate, they'd be lucky to get any time together before he had to head to the game. She eyed the bumper-to-bumper traffic in front of her. Enough of this madness. She scooped up her phone and fired up the GPS for an alternate route. Great, now she just needed to get to that exit 300 meters ahead.

Fifteen minutes later, she was still no further forward in the line. Screw it. She glanced in her rearview mirror and saw no other vehicles. She hated to be that guy, but desperate times. She swung the car onto the shoulder of the road and zipped up the line of traffic to the turnoff. As she rounded the corner onto the turnoff, she saw several cars had followed behind her. Okay, she didn't feel quite so bad about being a dick now since they'd followed suit.

Finally, on the new road, she zipped toward Pete's house. At 1:15, she pulled up to Pete's loft. She had barely put the car in park when her door was pulled open and Pete loomed over her.

"Thank god you're here." He reached across her and unhooked her seatbelt. Grabbing her hand, he pulled her out of the car and into his arms. His mouth was on her the second she stood upright.

"Fuck, Kendall." He breathed into her mouth. His firm hands wrapped around her waist, picking her up. She wrapped her legs around his hips, allowing him to carry her into his house.

His teeth scraped down the side of her neck. "Sorry, I know I'm being a bit of an asshole here."

She tilted her head to the side to allow him better access to her neck and moaned. "Don't apologize. I like it."

He kicked the door closed behind him and pressed her up against the door. "Why do you always smell so fucking good?" he growled. He pushed her shirt off her shoulder and licked his way towards her chest.

Her brain was on overload. She could barely compute what was happening. She'd gone from anxious and stressed to wanton in a heartbeat and her mind could barely keep up.

Kendall threaded her fingers through his hair and pulled his head back so she could look at his face. Chests heaving as they both sucked in a breath. His nostrils flared and he licked his lips as he stared back at her. His eyes were cloudy and turbulent with lust and something else she'd never seen before. Her heart raced. My god, the way he looked at her. It had to mean something. There was no way he could look at her like that and not feel the same way she did. She arched her hips and pressed her core against his hard cock. "Take me to bed, Pete."

His lips crashed against hers. His hand tightened around her ass and kneaded the flesh as he stalked towards the stairs.

"Put me down and I'll walk up the stairs," she grumbled.

"We've had this conversation before. I like carrying you. If you want to be helpful, you could ditch the shirt."

Kendall grabbed the hem of her sweater and peeled it over her head, and dropped it on the stairs as they ascended towards Pete's room.

A low groan rumbled from Pete's chest, and she followed his stare down to her chest. Her nipples beaded tightly against the lace of her bra, clearly visible beneath the sheer fabric.

She reached behind her back to get the clasp.

"No, leave it," Pete grunted.

"Really?"

"Definitely." He stopped on the step and pressed her against the wall. Dipping his head, he sucked her nipple into his mouth and dragged his teeth against it. As her nipple tightened, the lace scratched against her sensitive skin. "Holy shit," she groaned. Maybe he was onto something with leaving the bra on. The lace had felt so soft before, now it rubbed roughly against her nipple, making it hypersensitive. The contrast between Pete's hot mouth and the slightly raw feeling created by the lace felt amazing.

Pete spun her off the wall and quickly carried her up the final steps. In his bedroom, he set her down and followed her onto the mattress.

Needing to feel his weight on her, she dug her heels into his ass and pulled him tightly against her. Pete groaned and ground his hips into her. They had far too many clothes on. She reached down and pushed his track pants down and over his ass. Thank god he was dressed casually and not in jeans.

Pete pushed back, reaching down with one arm, he shoved his pants down further. The muscles in his arms flexed as he held himself above her. She ran her fingers down the ridges of his forearm. Loving the way the muscles quivered beneath her touch, she continued to stroke his arm.

He pulled her pants off and stared down at her body clad only in the lacy bra. "This first time is going to be fast. I promise to make it up to you after the game," he told her.

"Fast is good." She arched her back, and he grabbed her hips and pressed his cock against her heated core. "Fast is perfect," she moaned.

Pete bit back a groan. "Hold that thought." He leaned over and grabbed a condom from the bedside table and quickly sheathed himself. "Okay, where were we?"

Kendall reached down and grabbed his cock. She slid her hand up the shaft once, twice, loving the way Pete grit his teeth as he watched her hand slowly stroking his shaft. She pressed him to her entrance and wrapped her legs tightly around his waist. "I think we were about here," she murmured.

Pete grabbed her hips and pressed deeply in one firm thrust, causing them both to moan. Even as turned on as she was, it took a second to adjust to his size and she held him in place for a moment. Threading her hands into his hair, she pulled his mouth down to hers. His tongue dipped into her mouth and she sucked it inside. Pete's hands gripped her hips firmly. His fingers dug into her flesh as he fought to hold on to his control. She swiveled her hips and clenched her inner muscles, and Pete's head dropped back. "Jesus, Ken, you gotta stop or I'm not going to last at all."

"Good. I don't want you to last. I want you to fuck me hard like you want to."

His eyes whipped open and he stared down at her, hungry and wild. "Be careful what you ask for," he growled.

She squeezed her inner muscles again. "I know exactly what I'm asking for."

His mouth crashed down on hers. His tongue mimicked the motion of his cock as he thrust into her. Hard, fast. All she could do was hold on for the ride as he took what he wanted.

This was what she'd asked for, Pete undone, out of control because he needed her just as much as she needed him.

Pete pushed up on his knees, bringing her with him so her body was half up in the air. "Oh my god," she cried out. The new angle hit her in an incredible way, the friction of his pelvis hitting her clit as he thrust, adding a whole new dimension. She reached above her head and held onto the headboard to hold herself in place. There was no way she was losing this angle now that he'd hit it. "Don't stop," she begged.

Pete threw his head back and his hips jerked as he came.

Damn. She relaxed her hand from its grasp.

"Leave your hands there," Pete growled.

What was happening? She didn't think guys could keep going once they were done. Clearly, she was wrong.

Holding her in place with one arm, he reached down and pinched her clit as he continued to thrust into her.

"Oh my god," she groaned as her orgasm ripped through her. Spent, she flopped her arms onto the mattress. What a welcome.

Pete quickly went into the bathroom and returned a moment later. She pried her eyes open when he dropped onto the mattress beside her.

"I promise to do better when I get home from the game," he said as he placed a kiss against her shoulder.

"I don't think that's possible."

A slow, cocky grin spread across his face. "Just wait." He kissed her shoulder again. "Sorry, I have to head to the stadium for warm-up. I'll get back here as quickly as I can after the game."

"Good luck." She threaded her fingers through his hair and pulled him down for a kiss.

He groaned against her lips. "Damn, I have never wanted to call in sick for work before in my life."

She knew that feeling well. Kendall giggled. "Get to work. I'll be here when you get home."

He stared down at her for several seconds without saying anything, then finally nodded his head. Pushing off the bed, he glanced down at her. "Get some rest. I have plans for you tonight," he said and waggled his eyebrows.

"Promises, promises." Kendall winked. "Now get to work."

She watched him as he left the room. Glancing around Pete's bedroom, she sighed. This was where she belonged, and she was going to make him see that this weekend. Enough of this secretive friends with benefits garbage. She was going to prove to him just how good they could be together if he gave them a chance.

CHAPTER FOURTEEN

P ete glanced over at Kendall as she reached into the fridge on Sunday morning. What a weekend. He never would have thought he'd enjoy having someone in his space as much as he enjoyed having Kendall there. Growing up playing ball, he'd billeted at people's houses and roomed with teammates, and he'd always found the process somewhat painful. The communal space, the lack of privacy, it had always felt so invasive. Somehow, with Kendall, it was different.

She turned and handed him the blueberries and set the pint of raspberries on the island. "Quit slacking and get stirring that batter, mister. Those muffins aren't going to make themselves."

He eyed the recipe in front of him and the amount of sugar listed and raised his eyebrow as he looked at her skeptically. "How can you call them muffins? They are more like cupcakes."

Kendall narrowed her eyes and scowled at him. "Clearly they're muffins. They have crumble topping with oats. Everyone knows oats are breakfast food."

Pete snorted. "Yeah, oatmeal. Not sugar laden crumble."

"Just wait. You are going to eat your words when you taste these things."

He scooped the batter into the muffin tins and slid the tray into the oven. Turning, he glanced at Kendall. "We have twenty minutes," he said, and waggled his eyebrows at her.

He'd expected her to move towards him. Instead, she chewed her bottom lip nervously and then sat down on a stool at the island. "Can we maybe talk instead?"

"Uh, sure, what's up?" His stomach tensed at the look on her face. Anxiety streamed off her in waves. What the hell was going on?

She rang her hands together and glanced at him then back down at her hands. "So, um, I haven't really known how to bring this up."

"Shit, you're not pregnant, are you?" His heart pounded in his chest. Kendall was going to hate him. He'd fucked up her life just like he'd fucked up his parents.

"What? No. God." Kendall sat up straight on her stool. "Relax, it's nothing like that. But good to know how freaked out you would be if I was."

"Well, come on, we're not exactly in a position to have a baby. That's pretty much the exact opposite of casual."

Kendall leaned back on her stool and pinned him with a stare. "Is that still what you want?"

His shoulder muscles tensed. "What do you mean?"

"I mean, is that still what you want? Just something casual with me?"

He rubbed the back of his neck. "We talked about this. What else can we be?" His brain fought to come back online as he tried to process the conversation, but all he kept hearing was his dad's voice telling him what a stupid fuckup he was.

She shrugged. "I don't know. Like I said before, things can change."

Where was she going here? This was exactly what he was afraid of when they'd agreed to do this casual arrangement. "Spell it out for me Ken, what are we talking about?"

She worried her bottom lip between her teeth again, then squared her shoulders and made eye contact with him. "I didn't want to bring it up earlier because I wanted to enjoy the weekend, and I'm not sure what you are going to say when I tell you this."

"Spit it out," he growled.

"The reason I'm back here in San Diego is because they offered me Mark's job. So I'm here to decide if I want it."

"Mark's job, like the weeny in charge? That Mark?"

"Yeah."

"Wow, that's great. It would be a fantastic opportunity for you."

"Yep."

Shit, what did that mean for them if Kendall moved to the city? His gaze flashed back to her. "What are you asking?"

She stood up and walked towards him. Standing right in front of him, she placed her hands around his waist.

"I guess I'm asking if I moved here, would you want to try to have a real relationship with me?"

Fuck. He stepped back and her hands fell to her sides. "Um...we...uh," he stammered. He stepped to the other side of the island to put some space between them.

"We talked about this, Kendall. This was always supposed to be casual."

"Right, because I lived in Atlanta and you lived here, so it didn't make sense to be anything else." She rested her fingers on the edge of the counter. "But if I move here, there's no reason we couldn't try something else."

"Um, there's a huge reason we couldn't try something. Your brother would fucking kill me if he knew I was with you."

"No, he wouldn't," she grumbled.

"Have you met Ryan? He absolutely would." He ran his hand roughly through his hair. Why was she doing this? Why couldn't she just be happy with things the way they were? What they had was perfect. "We agreed if this happened between us Ryan would never know. Now you want me to fuck my friendship with your brother and mess up the season all so we can be openly fucking now that you're moving to town?"

Kendall sucked in a gasp at his harsh words.

"Shit," he muttered.

"Good to know where I stand," Kendall said. She turned and ran towards the stairs.

He swallowed down the wave of nausea that assaulted him as she sprinted from the room.

"Fuck," he yelled and slammed his hand down on the island.

Following Kendall, he jogged up the stairs. When he got to his bedroom, she had thrown her bag on his bed and was tossing clothing into it like they were on evacuation order and she only had seconds to get what she needed.

At the idea of her leaving, he felt sick again. "Where are you going?"

"Are you serious right now?" she screamed. Tears streamed down her cheeks and pain lanced through his chest. He'd made her cry. This was exactly why he'd wanted to remain casual. He'd always known he'd hurt her, and that was the last thing he'd ever wanted.

"Kendall, stop, look at me," he pleaded.

"Why?" she cried.

"I don't know...because I don't want things to end like this."

"Then stop being an asshole," she said as she spun towards him with her lace bra in her hand. The same bra she'd been wearing when she'd arrived on his doorstep on Friday night. How was it possible that in two days his entire world had changed so much?

"I'm not trying to be an asshole, Kendall. But we talked about this. I told you I'm not a forever guy. I told you this wasn't going anywhere."

"I know, but I thought that was before. How can you make love to me the way you do and not care about me?" she cried.

He took a deep breath and exhaled as he tried to formulate his thoughts. "It's not that I don't care about you, Kendall. I do. I'm just not willing to fuck up my friendship and my team for something temporary." Once she truly got to know him, she wouldn't stay. No one did.

"But why does it have to be temporary?" she whispered.

He dropped down onto the chair in the corner of the room. "Because that's who I am."

"No Pete, that's who you choose to be." She zipped up her bag. "Clearly I don't know you as well as I thought I did."

What the hell did that mean? "I'm exactly who I've always told you I am, Kendall. I never lied to you. I never made promises."

"Your body did."

"What does that mean? It was sex, Kendall. Sure, it was fucking fantastic, but it was sex."

"God, you really are an asshole." She slung her bag over her shoulder and stormed towards the door.

He stepped in front of her to block the door. "That's it? We're done talking?"

"There's nothing else to say. You've made yourself very clear. Now move." She pushed against his stomach, but he couldn't move. Fear held him in place. If she walked out that door, he was scared he'd never see her again.

"What about when we run into each other?" he asked.

"If I have my way, that will never happen."

"Kind of hard if you move to town," he told her. The idea of seeing her at Ryan's for team BBQ's and games and not being able to touch her was unbearable.

"Not as hard as you'd think. Now move." She pressed against his stomach again. This time, he moved to the side.

He followed her downstairs. What the hell was he supposed to do? He couldn't risk everything just to see if they could make this work.

Part of him wanted to beg her not to go, to say they'd figure this out. The other part worried that when she finally realized she was too good for him and left for good, he would have blown up his whole life for nothing, and then where would he be?

At the front door, Kendall turned around and faced him. God, she looked so fierce. Like a warrior with her hair wild, her face flushed from tears and anger, chest heaving. She'd never looked more beautiful.

He wanted nothing more than to wrap her in his arms and beg her not to go, but for how long? No, she was better off without him. The one thing he knew for sure in this world was that people didn't stay.

"I can't believe I was so wrong about you. I thought I could change your mind and convince you that there was more to you than you thought. But maybe you were right and I was the one who was blinded by a silly schoolgirl crush. Because the guy I thought you were is a fighter who never gives up on anything. The guy I'm looking at is a fucking pussy, and I don't need that."

She whipped open the front door and stormed out, slamming it shut behind her. He stood staring at the door, unable to move, until the smoke detector started beeping madly, pulling him out of his trance.

He ran over to the stove and pulled open the door. Smoke spilled out of the oven, filling the kitchen with the stench of burning blueberry muffins. He grabbed the tea towel and pulled the burned tray out. The heat instantly spread through the towel. He looked down at the muffins and yelled as he threw the tray violently against the wall. He slumped down on the floor with his back against the island. Charred muffin bits covered the kitchen, mocking him with the mess he'd made of things with Kendall.

It was just supposed to be a casual fling. So why did it feel like he had just burned the best thing in his life to the ground?

He dropped his head back with a thump against the island and closed his eyes. When he'd woken up this morning, he'd been flying high. He'd had an amazing weekend with Kendall. His team had won both games so far against Chicago and was hoping to sweep the series. He'd been feeling relaxed and confident. And now? His hand throbbed and he looked down at the angry red mark that slashed across his palm. *Even better.*

At least now, he'd have an excuse if he played like shit. He banged his head against the cupboard. What if he'd made a huge mistake in sending Kendall away?

He didn't know how long he'd been sitting there when Mooch slid up beside him and dragged his body along Pete's arm. He dropped his hand and scooped the cat up onto his lap. He rubbed Mooch's back, allowing the rhythmic purring to soothe his frayed nerves. He looked down at the cat, who was staring up at him. The look on Mooch's face said even the cat thought he was an idiot. Awesome. He glanced at the clock. Shit. He needed to get to the ball field.

Pushing himself up off the floor, he grabbed his bag from his home gym and made his way to the car.

Thirty minutes later, he eased his car into the stadium parking lot. Taking a deep breath, he exhaled and tried to slow his breathing down, forcing himself to follow his normal pregame ritual. After several deep breaths, he still wasn't feeling any better.

Knuckles wrapped on his window, and he glanced over to see Gonzo standing beside his car. Well, ready or not. He exhaled one last time, then forced himself to put on his game face and exit the car.

"What were you doing in there, Zip?" Gonzo asked.

"Nothing, just..." He shook his head. "Nothing." He slapped Gonzo on the back. "Are we making a sweep today?"

"You know it. I'm going to light Henderson up. It'll look like he's lobbing softballs."

Pete chuckled. "Big talk, Gonz, big talk."

"Well, we can't all be you Zip, but I'm going to make him weep today."

"Looking forward to seeing it," Pete replied as they walked down the hallway towards the dressing rooms.

Inside the dressing room, he dropped down onto the bench and rested his arms on his knees as he tried to get his head on straight.

"What's up with you today, man? You look like you're gonna cry or something," Ryan said.

If it wasn't for Ryan, he wouldn't be in this position. He wouldn't have had to worry about things with Kendall and they could have let things just play out. It was his fault he was feeling like this. "Fuck you." He glared at his closest friend on the team. Normally, he would talk to Ryan about this kind of thing, but he couldn't. The whole thing just sucked.

"What the fuck, dude? You on your rag or something," Ryan snarled.

The loud crack of a towel snapping followed by the high-pitched yelp out of Ryan's mouth had a smile cracking across Pete's lips. He glanced over at their trainer, Jessie, and grinned. "Guess you heard that, hey?" he asked, laughing as he watched Ryan rubbing the welt that was forming on the side of his ass.

"Hard not to." She pinned Ryan with a glare. "Listen, hotshot, I know you're used to women fawning all over themselves around you, but trust me, that comment wasn't only sexist, it was insensitive."

Ryan dipped his head down and mumbled, "Sorry, Jess."

"Don't apologize to me. Apologize to your friend," she ordered.

"It actually hurt my feelings," Pete said, trying hard not to laugh when Ryan's eyes narrowed as he glared at Pete.

"Fuck you," Ryan replied.

Pete rubbed his chest. "Ouch, that's not helping." He glanced over at her. "Jessie, he's not being very nice."

She rolled her eyes. "Oh my god, you two, grow-up. Seriously though, Pete, are you okay? You seem a bit off."

Trying to center himself so he could get his head out of his ass, he flexed his hands. Pain from his burn ran across his palm, giving him the perfect excuse for his sour mood. "Yeah, fine, just burned my hand this morning. It's nothing."

Jessie kneeled down beside him. "Let me see."

He opened his hand, exposing the angry red blister.

"Shit, Pete, that looks like it hurts." She winced.

"It's no big deal." He shrugged. It was nothing compared to what was going on inside his head.

"Come on, let's get it wrapped up so you don't rip it open and get it infected," she told him.

"Why didn't you say you were hurt?" Ryan asked.

"Because it's nothing."

"Okay, well, get it fixed up, then get your head on straight. You need to be on your game out there today," Ryan ordered.

"When am I not?" Pete growled.

Ryan stared at him so long Pete felt like he had a neon sign flashing over his head that said *Kendall, Kendall, Kendall*.

"Get fixed up, and Jessie, make sure you get the head out of his ass while he's back there, all right?"

Jessie snickered. "Not in my job description. I think that's more your job, Pitch."

Turning to Pete, she said, "Come on, let's get you fixed up."

Following her towards the training room, he looked down at the angry blister that covered his entire palm. If only fixing up what was wrong was as easy as slapping some protective wrap on. It would take a hell of a lot more than that to fix what he'd broken.

CHAPTER FIFTEEN

Monday night after the game, Ryan dropped down onto the stool beside him. "Fuck, I need a beer." He raised his arm to flag down the server.

"Hey, how you doing?" Ryan said to the server. "Can I grab an Arrogant Bastard from you when you get a chance?"

Pete snorted beside him. "Why does it only sound so funny when you order that beer?"

"Because you're twelve," Ryan replied.

"I might have to see some ID then," the server teased.

"Right," Pete laughed.

She flicked her hair over her shoulder, pushed out her hip, and leaned against the table. The movement pressed her breasts up even higher. His gaze flicked down to her chest, then back up. *Eh, Kendall's were better.*

She smiled. "Can I get either of you anything else?"

"Nah, I think we're good," Ryan replied.

"Okay, my name's Becca, so just holler if you need me." Her gaze trailed over both of them flirtatiously. Pete couldn't have said which of them she was interested in or if it really didn't matter to her. Normally he would have flirted back with the sexy waitress, but he had zero interest in any woman but Kendall, and he couldn't have her. What a mess.

"What's going on? Why are your panties in such a twist?" Pete asked.

Ryan rolled his shoulders. "Ah, my sister."

Pete's back straightened at the mention of Kendall. "What about her?"

The server came back and set the beer on the table in front of Ryan. Pete flicked an annoyed look at her as she lingered near their table. Fuck. Could she just leave already? He needed to know what was wrong with Kendall.

"Your sister?" Pete prodded.

"Yeah," Ryan sighed. "Last night I could hear her crying in her room." He rubbed his hand across his forehead, pushing his ball cap up awkwardly, then adjusting it back in place. "So, I forced her to let me in so we could talk."

Pete's stomach knotted. Fuck, he hated this situation they were in. "Why was she crying?"

"Some fucking guy." Ryan took a long swig of his beer. "I didn't even know she was seeing anyone. She hadn't mentioned him to me when she got here."

"What about the guy? What'd she say?" Nerves raced through him. He rubbed his hands against his thighs. Jesus, maybe Ryan was right and he really was twelve. His freaking palms were starting to sweat.

"Fucking asshole said she wasn't worth fighting for," Ryan snarled.

Pete's spine straightened. "What? He didn't say that."

"That's what she said," Ryan replied.

What the actual fuck? That's definitely not what he said. "Maybe she just misunderstood him," Pete said.

Ryan shrugged. "She seemed pretty clear on things." He leaned back in his chair and glanced around the bar. "The waitress is pretty hot," Ryan said as he continued to watch her move around the pub.

"Yeah, she's fine. So Kendall?" he prodded.

"Right, yeah... man, I hate seeing my baby sister cry. I want to rip the fucking guy's head off, but she won't tell me who he is."

"She wouldn't tell you who he was, but she was really upset they weren't going to be together?"

"Yeah. She said she was crazy about him, but there was some bullshit that made things tricky to be together, and he didn't think she was worth fighting for."

"Maybe it had nothing to do with her not being worth it. Maybe he's not," Pete replied. God, he hated that Kendall thought it was because she didn't matter that he'd said they should cool things down. That wasn't it at all.

"He's definitely not worth it. He's a fucking pussy," Ryan growled.

"I'm sure he's not a pussy," Pete grumbled.

"What kind of fucking guy pulls the whole it's not you it's me bullshit? Things are too complicated and messy, waa waa waa," Ryan fake whined. "Pussy."

Jesus, that was harsh. He wasn't a fucking pussy. It had nothing to do with that. "Maybe the guy just didn't feel good enough for her."

Ryan rolled his eyes. "Yeah. Or maybe he was just some asshole who wanted to get laid and then didn't want to stick around after." Ryan puffed up his chest and rolled his shoulders. "I'd fucking rip him apart if I knew who he was. My sister was a mess, man. Now she's not sure if she wants to accept this promotion." He shook his head. "I've never seen her like that before."

Pete rubbed his hand across his face, his palm scraping against the stubble. God, never in a million years had he imagined Kendall felt so strongly about him. I mean, he knew the chemistry was crazy between them, but she'd seemed so aloof most of the time when they'd talked. She'd wanted to keep things casual just as much as he had right up until this past weekend. He'd thought maybe he'd imagined the connection between them most of the time. Hell, she'd even been dating other guys. But what if what Ryan was saying was true, and she really felt exactly the same as him? He looked at Ryan. Unfortunately, that didn't change the fact that he would never be good enough for her.

"Your sister is amazing. The guy probably didn't deserve her," Pete said.

"Obviously he doesn't if he's not willing to fight for her. Ken is strong. She needs a real man, not one of those posers she normally goes for." Ryan lifted his beer to his mouth and looked at Pete. "How come you never went after my sister?"

"What? What do you mean, how come I never went after her?"

"I don't know. For a while there, I thought maybe you might be interested," Ryan shrugged.

"Would you have been okay with it if I was? When we were younger, you said you'd kill me if I even looked at your sister."

"Yeah, but we were kids then and you were a frickin' dog," Ryan replied.

"I haven't been much better in the past few years." He was ashamed to admit that he wasn't proud of the man he'd become. The fame of being a professional athlete had gone to his head and he'd taken advantage of all the lifestyle had to offer. And until Kendall had come back into his life, he hadn't realized how empty that all was.

"No, but you wouldn't be like that with my sister," Ryan said confidently. "Because I'd fucking kill you."

"You'd be okay with me dating her?"

"Yeah, I mean, if you actually wanted to date her and not just, you know.... act like you do normally." Ryan stared at him across the table and Pete fought not to squirm.

"Are you interested in dating my sister?"

Pete swallowed and took a deep breath. "Yeah...yeah I am."

Ryan nodded. "Okay. I don't know if she'd date you, though. You can be a bit of a dog."

Pete lowered his head. "I wouldn't be that way with Kendall. She deserves better than that."

"Fuck yeah, she does," Ryan responded. "Maybe you could help her get over this asshole."

Pete raised his head and looked Ryan in the eyes. "What if I said I was the asshole who Kendall was talking about?"

"What?" Ryan snarled. "You fucked my sister?" he roared.

Before Pete even had time to process anything, a fist connected with his face, knocking him off his chair. His elbow rammed against the floor. Pain ripped through his cheekbone and he tried to push up off the floor to protect himself. His elbow buckled as a monster zinger raced up his arm. The funny bone hit from hell. Holy shit, that fucking hurt.

He glanced up at Ryan, towering over him. "You fucker," Ryan growled.

Pete stood up and squared off with Ryan. "I thought you said you were fine with me dating your sister."

"I was. But you fucking hurt her, man." Anger radiated off Ryan. "You made her cry." Ryan glared at him. "I didn't think you'd hurt her when I said you could ask her out, but you didn't just hurt her, you destroyed her."

Pete slumped against the chair. "I know, and it kills me. I'm crazy about her, Ry. She's..." He sighed. "She's everything."

"Then why did you tell her she wasn't worth fighting for?" Ryan snapped.

"I didn't. I said I wasn't worth it." He paused. He really didn't want to have this conversation here in the pub with people watching them. "Can we sit?" he asked.

Ryan sat back down on his chair and Pete slid into his. His cheek throbbed and he rolled his neck. Son of a bitch, Ryan could throw a punch.

"What did you say to Kendall?" Ryan asked.

"I told her that your friendship was important to me."

"Not important enough to keep your hands to yourself," Ryan grumbled.

"I guess not, no. But...she's just...I don't know how to explain it, man. She's..." Pete glanced at Ryan. Uncomfortable with the scrutiny, he looked down at the table. "She's..."

"Everything?" Ryan asked.

"Yeah." He looked up at the ceiling. God, this was horrifying. "Your sister is amazing. She's beautiful, she's smart, and god she makes me laugh when we're together."

"Why did you break up with her?" Ryan pressed him.

"Because she deserves better than me. I'm thirty years old and I've never been in a committed relationship. My track record sucks." He flexed his arm out to loosen the residual pain in his funny bone. "I'm one injury away from losing my career, and I have no backup plan. Baseball is it for me."

"Is your arm okay?" Ryan chewed his bottom lip as he looked at Pete's arm.

"What? Yeah, it's fine, just banged it. It's nothing. That's not what I'm saying. But I mean look at me. You at least went to university. You have a backup plan. I don't." He blew out a breath. "Your sister should be with someone smart, someone like a doctor or a lawyer or something. She can do so much better than a guy like me."

"If I thought you weren't good enough for my sister, I wouldn't have said you could ask her out," Ryan told him.

"Yeah, why did you say that?"

"You don't have a fancy degree, but you're one of the best guys I know. And if you decided you want to be with someone, you'd move heaven and earth to make them happy."

"You think?" God, he hated how needy he sounded by asking that.

"Yeah. Hell man, you adopted a freaking cat and spent a small fortune on his vet bills, and you hate cats."

"Well, that's Mooch, he's not a regular cat," Pete replied.

"That's my point. You have a huge heart. You've been one of my best friends since we were fourteen years old. I know you. I trust you." He titled his head to the side as he stared at Pete. "If Kendall will have you back, you have my blessing."

Pete grinned. "Really?"

"Of course." Ryan winced, then laughed. "But you're going to have your work cut out for you. Kendall is not easy. She's pissed and she's hurt and that girl can carry a grudge. She still talks about the time I wrecked her precious stuffed animal when she was eight."

Ryan leaned back in his chair and crossed his arms over his chest. "Good luck." Ryan scanned Pete's face and grimaced. "You might want to put some ice on that." He pointed to Pete's face. "You're starting to swell shut."

"Shit." He gingerly touched his eye. Okay, yeah, that hurt. Glancing around for the server, he waved her over when he caught her attention. "Any chance I could grab a little bag of ice?"

She glanced at Pete's eye, then over at Ryan. "You two kiss and make up?"

"Yeah, we're good," Pete told her.

"I'll be right back with some ice. Don't want your pretty face to be all marked up," she mocked.

Pete glanced over at Ryan and smirked. "I think we're going to need to leave her a big tip."

Resting his elbows on the table, Ryan watched Pete with the same focused attention he gave when he was staring down a batter. It was tempting to squirm under the scrutiny.

"You got a plan for how to get my sister back?"

"I don't have the first fucking clue. I kind of just thought I'd show up at your place. Tell her I fucked up and beg her to give me a chance."

Ryan pursed his lips and nodded his head slowly. "That could work. But I doubt it will be that easy."

The server unceremoniously dropped a ziplock bag filled with ice on the table and walked away before he even got a chance to say thank you. He placed the bag of ice against his swollen face and sucked in a breath.

"Sorry about that, man. I hope it's not too swollen for Wednesday's game," Ryan said. "I should have punched you in the gut instead."

"That's fair. I deserved it." He rolled his neck back and forth. Man, it was bad enough getting punched in the face, but the fact that his neck felt like he had whiplash was kind of adding insult to injury. But if a bit of a headache and a bruised face were what it took to be with Kendall, he'd take that all day long. "It'll be fine. I'll keep it iced."

He shoved back from the table. "If it's okay with you, I'm going to take off and see if I can talk to Kendall."

"Good luck," Ryan mumbled.

"Do you mind giving us some time before you come home? I really would rather not beg in front of you if I don't have to."

"No problem. Just don't, like, have sex or anything in my house, please. It's bad enough to think of you dating my sister without having to come home to that."

"Hopefully that's something I have to think about," he said before he turned and walked towards the door. At this point, he was just hoping she'd answer the door when he arrived.

CHAPTER
SIXTEEN

K endall lay on the couch with a bag of chips and a box of Kleenex and scrolled through the channels looking for something that would take her mind off Pete. She paused when she got to a reality TV show with a couple arguing loudly with each other. The woman was screaming about the man not understanding what commitment really meant. "You tell him, sister," Kendall cheered.

The man on the screen slowly slid towards the woman and put a stupid look on his face and said, "Baby, you know you're the only woman that I want to be with." Kendall screamed and threw the tissue box at the screen.

God, women could be so stupid. She flicked the remote. Next.

Digging her hand into the chip bag, she paused when the doorbell rang. She peered down at herself. Dressed in her brother's baggy sweats with chip dust on her hands, she could just imagine what a train wreck her face looked like. Freakin' fantastic. Ryan wasn't home, so she was probably going to have to make polite conversation with whoever was at the door for him. What kind of person just pops by on a Monday night unannounced?

"Ugh," she groaned as she slid off the couch. She glanced down at the crumbs and tissues on the sofa where she'd been sitting. Okay, yeah, that was gross. She needed to get her shit together. It was one thing to cry over a guy, it was another to let herself slide into whatever the hell this was.

She smoothed her hair and walked towards the front door. With her hand on the doorknob, she paused and took a deep breath, then exhaled. She opened the door and immediately wanted to slam it shut when she saw Pete on the other side. Why didn't she look to see who it was before she answered?

"Ryan's not here."

"Yeah, I know. I just saw him. I came to see you," he said as he stepped toward her.

Oh god, his eye. She clenched her hand to stop herself from reaching out to soothe his swollen face. "Is that what happened to your face?"

"Yep."

"Guess you were right about how he'd react about us."

"No, not really."

"What do you mean?" she asked.

"This isn't because we got together, it's because I hurt you."

"So, you were all worried for nothing?"

He sighed deeply and ran his fingers through his hair. "Can I come in so we can talk?"

Kendall dropped her hand from the door and stepped back. Turning on her heel, she walked towards the living room. When she walked into the room, she pulled up short. Shoot, she'd forgotten about her wallowing mess when she'd led him to this room. Oh well, screw him. He broke her heart, let him see what that looked like.

Pete glanced down at the messy couch, winced, then sat gingerly on the edge of one of the single chairs in the room.

She pushed her blanket off to the side and sat down in the clean space on the sofa. "Why are you here, Pete?"

"I was hoping we could talk."

"About what?"

"Us."

"There is no us. So...again why are you here?"

Pete leaned forward, resting his elbows on his knees. "Ken, I fucked up. I got scared and pushed you away."

Unwilling to give him an inch, she stared back at him and bobbed her head to encourage him to continue.

"Have you decided if you are taking the job or not?"

"I don't see how that's any of your concern."

"Well, I was kind of hoping we could maybe try dating like you wanted."

"Like I wanted? Right," she scoffed. Because he'd made it abundantly clear that's not what he wanted. "What's changed? Why are you interested in dating now?"

He touched his swollen eye. "Well, like I said, Ryan and I talked."

"Oh, so now that my brother has given his blessing, it's okay to want me?" She shook her head. "Fuck you, Pete."

He stood up, walked toward her, and sat down on the coffee table. She shifted back on the couch and pulled her knees up to her chest to put some distance between them. Being so close to him, but emotionally so far apart, tore at her, leaving her feeling raw and vulnerable. She scooped the blanket off the cushion and pulled it over her lap like a shield.

"That's not what I meant. I just meant Ryan and I talked, so he knows about us."

"There is no us, Pete. You made that painfully clear to me already."

He reached his hand towards her, and she flinched back. If she allowed him to touch her, she'd probably cave. She had zero willpower when it came to this man.

"Come on, Kendall. What do you want me to say? I told you I know I messed up. I want us to figure this out."

"Okay, so what changed?"

"Like I said, Ryan and I talked and he's okay with us dating."

"Oh yeah, no, I got that part. Again, what's changed?"

Pete's forehead wrinkled in confusion when he looked at her. "What do you mean?"

"I mean, who cares if my brother knows?" she growled. "Are you seriously telling me the thing that stood between us dating and you breaking my heart was Ryan's approval?"

"Umm..." he stammered.

"Seriously?"

"I don't get why you're mad. You knew when we started this thing between us that my friendship with Ryan was important to me."

"Yep. You made that pretty clear." Pissed, she clenched her teeth and sucked in a breath. The tension made a small squeaking sound slide out of her mouth. Like even the air was afraid to move.

"What's happening here, Kendall? I thought you'd be happy. I thought this was what you wanted for me to talk to Ryan and for us to be together. I did that. I don't understand why you're pissed off."

"Okay, and if Ryan had said he wasn't okay with this. Would you be here?"

He looked down at his hands and raised his shoulders in that universal cop out sign of who knows. "I'm not sure," he said quietly.

"Right." She stood up off the couch. "You can leave now."

He jumped up. "What? That's it? We're done. All because I don't know what I would have said if Ryan didn't want us together." He stared at her as he sucked in a breath. His chest rising and falling like he was fighting for control. "I fucking risked my friendship with him to tell him about us. That should mean something."

"It does." Tears welled up behind her eyes. "It just doesn't mean enough."

"What the fuck does that mean?" he growled.

She tilted her head up to the ceiling and took a deep breath to stave off the tears that were trying their best to fall. She lowered her head and looked at Pete. His face was filled with so many emotions as he stared back at her. Anger, confusion, longing.

A huge part of her wanted to just forgive him. To wrap her arms around him and say they'd figure it out. But she couldn't do that. "You need to go," she whispered, unable to stop the tears from sliding down her face.

Pete grabbed her arm. "No, Kendall, talk to me." He brushed the tear that dripped down her cheek. "This isn't what you want. I know how much you care about me. Let's figure this out."

"There's nothing to figure out." Her eyes burned with tears as she looked at his face. She sniffed and shook her head. "I can't be second place. Not in this." She bit her top lip as she tried to get her emotions under control.

"God, you're not," Pete said as he stepped closer to her and tried to pull her into his arms.

She pushed against his chest and moved away from him. "That's the problem though, Pete. I am. I have been in Ryan's shadow my entire life." She paused. "Never good enough, always being compared to him and falling short." She angrily wiped the tears from her face. "I refuse to do that when it comes to this."

"You wouldn't be," Pete said.

Trying to draw on some kind of inner strength she wasn't feeling, she took a deep breath. "I would. I want the man I'm with to say fuck everyone and everything. I love this girl and I will do whatever it takes to be with her."

"That's what I'm doing," he growled.

"No, it's not. What you're doing is saying I want to be with her if it's okay with Ryan and if it's not, then.... who knows?" She shrugged her shoulders, mocking his earlier gesture.

"That's not fair, Kendall. This situation is complicated. Ryan isn't just my friend, he's my teammate. We work together every day and if things between us are tense, it can fuck up the flow of the entire team."

"No, I get that. Believe me, I grew up having the importance of baseball drilled into me."

"So..." He raised his hands in question. "It's complicated. I'm not saying we wouldn't still be together if Ryan didn't want us to be. I'm just saying I don't know."

She smiled sadly. "I want someone who knows. Who looks at me and says nothing will stand in the way of being with me. I think I deserve that."

"You deserve the best, Ken."

"And unfortunately, that's not you." As much as it hurt her to say it, she knew she'd never be first with Pete. "Ryan is always going to be more important to you than me."

"That's not fair. Ryan and I have been through a lot together. He's been with me through some pretty hard stuff, and I'm not just going to throw that away on a temporary girlfriend, no matter who she is."

Her chest tightened like it was being crushed between a vise. Why couldn't he see how great they could be together? Despite everything, he still just saw her as temporary. He would never see her as the kind of woman he'd settle down with, so no wonder Ryan came first. Not only was she second best behind her brother, she was second best behind some mystical dream girl he thought he'd end up with. That hurt even more.

"So you still just see us as temporary?"

"I don't know. I see every relationship as temporary. It's not personal."

"No Pete, that's where you're wrong. It's very personal."

He rolled his eyes. "You don't have to take everything I say so literally. I'm not a word guy like you. I'm just a dumb jock. I'm not good at this stuff."

"Words are important, Pete, no matter who is saying them. But you're right. If this is just going to be something temporary, then there's really no point in continuing what we are doing because it's not going anywhere."

She took a deep breath, then squared her shoulders to face him. "I don't think there's anything left to say, Pete. Clearly, we both want different things. I'm a forever kind of girl, but I'm not your forever girl. This is hard enough as it is without dragging things out."

She walked towards the door, silently encouraging him to follow. "I'm glad you and Ryan worked things out. You should get home and ice your face so you can play on Wednesday."

"Fuck the game," he growled.

"Pete, don't. Trust me, you'll go home, ice your face and realize I did you a favor by letting you off the hook."

He pressed against her shoulder to try to force her to look at him. Raising her head, tears burned behind her eyes as she looked at him and the lost expression on his face. It would be so easy to just accept the crumbs he was offering. To bask in what he was willing to give her of himself, knowing all the while it was just a matter of time before he moved onto something better because she wasn't his dream girl, despite how badly she wanted to be.

Steeling herself to stay strong, she said, "I'm sorry, Pete, but it's too hard to keep going like we are. I love you and you're never going to love me the way I want."

"How can you say you love me already? We've barely been dating."

"That's what I'm talking about. I do love you. I know that down to my soul. The fact that you don't know how you feel about me is exactly why we're done here." She blinked back her tears. "I'm really fucking tired of being second choice. I'm not doing this anymore. I'm not waiting around, hoping one day you'll love me like I love you," she cried. "Just let me go, Pete. Let me move on and find someone who will be able to love me like I need."

He cupped the side of her face and pressed a kiss against her forehead. "I'm sorry, Peanut. I wish I could be the guy you want me to be." With that, he turned on his heel and walked out the front door.

The second she closed the door, she slid to the floor, resting her back against it and let the tears flow freely. She had thought she would have been all cried out after the past few days, but apparently, she still had plenty left to give.

CHAPTER SEVENTEEN

Pete slung his bag over his shoulder and walked towards the airport check-in. Maybe being away from San Diego for the next week would help him get his head on straight. Last night with Kendall had been brutal. When he'd gotten home, he'd pulled out a bottle of Jack and hadn't stopped until he passed out.

As he slid up to the counter and pulled out his ticket, the counter attendant took one look at him and winced. "What's the other guy look like?" she asked.

"A hell of a lot better than I do," he admitted. Passing out instead of icing his eye hadn't helped any. This morning when he woke up, it was just a little slit he could barely see out of. Thankfully, they didn't actually play until tomorrow, so hopefully by then the swelling would have gone down. He grabbed his boarding pass and made his way through security. Walking up to the gate, he took a deep breath as he mentally prepared himself to face his teammates and the ribbing that was surely coming his way based on the way he knew he looked.

There were no boundaries between teammates, which sometimes was a great thing. Days like today, he couldn't think of anything worse. He hiked his carryon higher on his shoulder and wandered up to the guys. Without saying a word, he dropped into an empty seat and pulled his hat over his eyes, and pretended he wanted to sleep. He'd barely got himself adjusted when he felt someone plop into the seat beside him.

"What's doing, Zip?"

"Of course, Gonzo would be the one to come bug him. "Nothing, just tired."

His hat was pulled off his face and Gonzo reared back and covered his mouth with his hand. "Woah, Zip, what the hell happened?"

Pete groaned as Gonzo's loud voice drew the attention of several other guys, drawing a crowd around them. He grabbed his hat back from Gonzo and pulled it down low over his eyes. "Nothing," he objected.

A firm hand clasped against his shoulder. "I punched him," Ryan's deep voice cut through the team.

"Seriously?" Gonzo asked.

"Yeah. He should have kept his dick in his pants."

Pete tilted his head back and scowled at Ryan. "Really?" he asked. So much for bygones. He couldn't believe Ryan was really going to air their dirty laundry out here in front of everyone.

"What? It's true. At least be man enough to own it."

Feeling uncomfortable with the height difference between them, he stood up and looked Ryan in the eye. "I thought we were good?"

"We are, but it doesn't change why I punched you. You deserved it." Ryan smirked. "Guess you didn't take my advice on the ice."

He pulled his hat down further on his brow, covering the offensive mark. "I got busy."

"Did you guys make up?"

"What? You don't know?"

"How would I know? I haven't seen her. Her door was closed when I got home, and she'd already left for work when I got up."

"Whoa, whoa, whoa, who are we talking about here?" Gonzo asked.

"My sister," Ryan replied.

"Holy shit, you fucked Graves' sister?" Anderson asked.

Pete spun around and glared at the catcher. "Who invited you to this conversation, Andy?"

Anderson raised his hands and stepped back. "Don't get all pissy with me because you got your ass kicked by a pitcher."

Ryan turned towards Anderson. As he stared down at the other man, his chest puffed, and he appeared to grow taller right before their eyes. "Watch it, dickhead, or I'll kick your ass too."

"Sorry. I just meant, you normally are the calmest, most controlled guy on the field. It surprised me that you hit him."

"Did you miss the part where I said it was my sister?"

Anderson made an exaggerated face and looked at Pete and shook his head. "Dude, everyone knows you don't fuck your friend's sister."

"Can you fuck off now, please?" Pete asked.

The flight attendant's voice came over the loudspeaker to let them know they were now boarding. "Thank god," Pete mumbled.

He found his seat and dropped into it, and a moment later, Ryan slid into the seat beside him. "Are you kidding me?" Pete asked.

"Nope," Ryan replied as he buckled himself into his seat, then turned to face Pete. "So, how'd it go last night?"

"Umm...not well." He clenched his jaw and looked out the window, so he didn't have to make eye contact with his friend. What had he been thinking drinking last night? Sure, it had helped in the moment, but now he felt like he'd been run over by a truck and his brain was slow and muddled. Definitely not up to the task of having a heart to heart with Kendall's brother.

Holy shit, when had Ryan become Kendall's brother in his mind instead of her being Ryan's sister?

"Ok, what does that mean? Are you guys back together?"

"Not even close," Pete muttered. He placed his hand over his queasy stomach and eyed the barf bag in front of him. *God, please don't let me need to use that.*

"Did you talk to her?"

"I tried, but she wasn't too interested in what I had to say."

"That doesn't sound like Kendall."

"Well, maybe you don't know your sister as well as you think you do," Pete accused.

"Clearly. So, explain it to me. What happened that she wasn't willing to talk to you?"

He sighed and scrubbed his hand over his face, wincing when his palm hit his swollen eye. "Basically, she asked if I'd be there if you had a problem with us being together and I said I didn't know."

Ryan reared back. "What the fuck? How the fuck can you not know if you'd want to be with her?"

"What? It wasn't an issue, so it didn't matter."

"Of course it fucking matters. Are you telling me if I had said no, you would have walked away?"

"I don't know."

"Jesus," Ryan muttered. "Then maybe you don't deserve the chance to date my sister. I can't fucking believe you."

"What? What's your problem?"

"You're fucking lucky we're on this plane or I'd kick your ass again," Ryan growled.

"Are you kidding me? Now you're mad too?"

"You can't be that clueless, Pete." Ryan stared back at him like he was a moron. The disappointment and disdain on Ryan's face was exactly what Pete had been afraid of when he'd told Ryan about Kendall.

"Obviously I am. Yesterday you were fine with my pursuing things with Kendall and now you aren't?"

"Yesterday, I thought you were serious about her. Today I think you're like every other asshole and not at all the guy I thought you were. I don't even know you."

"You know me just fine." Pete's body pulled tight as he fought to stay in control. They really didn't need the entire team descending on them for this conversation.

"It never occurred to me you'd make a move on her if you weren't serious. I mean, why would you risk fucking up our friendship if she wasn't important? It doesn't make sense. You know how protective I am of her. Honestly, I didn't think you'd even glance her way if you didn't want a future with her. That's not who I thought you were." Ryan crossed his arms across his chest and stared forward, shaking his head.

Pete played over what Ryan said over and over in his mind. Was Ryan right? Had he been crazy about Kendall all along? Is that why he'd been willing to risk everything? Memories of Kendall played through his mind like a movie. All the key moments she'd been there to celebrate with him. She'd always been there in the background, silently supporting him. How clearly he could picture her shy smile, the encouraging nods he'd gone out of his way to seek out at every opportunity.

Holy shit.

Uncomfortable with the revelation, he shifted in his seat. "You weren't wrong about me. I wouldn't have fucked up our friendship over just anyone, but your sister isn't just anyone."

"Then wouldn't you have fought for her if I said no?"

"Of course I would have," Pete admitted.

"Okay, so why did you say you didn't know?"

He squirmed in his seat. What the hell was he supposed to say? It's not like he could admit to his friend that he was worried he wasn't good enough. That he understood Kendall's insecurities because he had them, too. "I really should be having this conversation with your sister, not you."

"Yeah, well, you aren't getting near her again until you pass me. So make it good."

He exhaled a shaky breath. "It wasn't that I wouldn't pick her or that she isn't worth fighting for because god knows she is. I just...shit," he mumbled. Pete pressed his tongue against the inside of his mouth, then filled his cheeks with air and let it out. "I wasn't sure I was."

"Don't be stupid. I told you already I think you guys would be great together."

"Yeah, but if you hadn't I wasn't sure what Kendall would pick."

"So you just chicken-shitted it by cutting first?"

"Yeah, I guess so."

"You're an idiot. My sister deserves someone who's willing to fight for her, man. Someone who's willing to humiliate himself if need be."

Pete sat up straight in his chair. "You just gave me a great idea of how to get her back."

"What's that?"

"Nope, not telling you until I work out the details, because you'd mock me mercilessly if I can't make it work."

"Okay, but like I said before, it better be good."

"Believe me, it will be." He grabbed his phone and quickly typed in a text to his agent that they needed to talk and hit send, praying it would go through the second he was out of airplane mode.

He turned to Ryan. "Thanks man. I appreciate the ass kick."

"Anytime. Knowing my sister, I'm sure it won't be the last time you need to hash things out."

Pete nervously tapped on his thigh. For the first time in his life, he hated their travel schedule. He wouldn't be able to see Kendall again until they got back to town on Sunday night and by then, who knows what she may have convinced herself of.

"Do you think Kendall will turn down the job in San Diego because of me?"

Ryan's brow lifted in thought. "I don't think so. She's usually pretty levelheaded, but she's always been a bit funny when it comes to you, so who knows?"

"What do you mean, she's always been funny about me?"

"Oh, come on, she did the dumbest things when she was younger to get your attention for all the good it did her."

"You knew about her crush? How did I miss it?"

"She was pretty annoying. You probably blocked it out." Ryan laughed.

"Maybe," he mumbled. Would he have been interested if he'd known? Probably not. He was pretty self-absorbed at the time. If he wasn't getting laid, he wasn't interested. God, he'd been an asshole back then. Hell, he was an asshole yesterday. But he was the asshole Kendall claimed to love and he would do anything to win her back because he definitely didn't find her annoying now.

Sunday night, Kendall stood in the kitchen stirring pasta sauce when Ryan arrived home.

"Smells good. Is that spaghetti?" Ryan asked as he pulled a stool out from the island and dropped onto it.

"Yeah, I figured you might be hungry after the game today. Tough loss."

"We should never have lost today. Pete was off his game the whole road-trip. Can you please take pity on the man and take him back so he can get his head out of his ass?"

"He did fine. He missed one ball." There was no way she was letting her brother blame their loss on her. If Pete didn't have his head on straight, that was Pete's problem, not hers.

"He didn't just miss the ball, it was an error that cost us the game."

"Oh my god, could you be more dramatic?" Kendall rolled her eyes. "That error let one run in. If that was the difference between winning and losing, I'd say that's on the team, not one player. What happened to baseball being a team sport?"

"Why are you defending him? I thought you hated him."

"I never said I hated him. Hell, I never said anything to you about him." Kendall turned back to the stove and looked down at the pot of sauce. She gave it one final stir, then set the spoon down. "It just needs to simmer for a bit. If you want to shower and get cleaned up by the time you get out, we should be ready to eat."

"So, we just aren't going to talk about Pete still?" Ryan pressed.

Kendall dropped her head. "I'd rather not, if at all possible. There's not much to talk about."

"Of course there is. He's crazy about you Ken, he said you aren't returning his texts or his calls."

"There's nothing to talk about. It's not going anywhere. Why delay the inevitable?"

"Who says it can't go anywhere?"

"It was just a casual fling, Ry. It didn't mean anything to him."

"Trust me, Ken, he wouldn't be behaving the way he is if it was just casual. I've seen Pete casual. This is not it."

"Well, it wasn't serious either."

Ryan walked to the fridge and pulled out a couple of beers and handed one to Kendall. "But it was serious for Pete."

"Did he say that?" Kendall's chest knotted as she waited for Ryan's response. What had Pete told her brother about them?

Ryan took a long pull of his beer, then sat back down on the stool. "What did Pete tell you about growing up?"

"Not much. Why?"

Ryan grabbed a napkin out of the holder in the middle of the island and wiped a water spot, then spun the napkin around and around in front of him.

"Oh, my god, spit it out, would you?" Kendall groaned.

"It's just, things for Pete were different than they were for us growing up. We had mom and dad and enough money to pay for everything. That wasn't the same for him."

"Okay, what does that have to do with anything?"

"Do you remember when Pete drove down after the draft and we all just laid up on the roof all night, looking at the stars and daydreaming about the future?"

"Of course I do." That night had been etched in her teenage brain because she'd lain beside Pete on the roof. Normally she was beside her brother, but that night she'd been beside Pete. She hadn't contributed a single thing to the conversation because her tongue had been glued to the roof of her mouth, but she'd been there.

"His dad showed up at the draft."

"Okay?" Where was he going with this?

"Pete's dad isn't a great guy."

"I thought he didn't have much to do with him."

"He doesn't. Before that night, he hadn't seen or heard from him in over a decade." Ryan spun the napkin around and around on the island as if deep in thought. "He saw Pete's draft as his meal ticket and when that didn't pan out the way he hoped, he was a bit of an asshole."

"How so?" Dread pooled in her stomach.

"He threatened to do a tell-all about Pete's mom and their life."

"What could he possibly say? From everything Pete has said, his mom is a saint."

"Yeah, that's the impression I always had too, but when it comes to tabloids, it doesn't always have to be the truth. From everything he's told me, Pete was a scrappy guy. The other kids weren't always nice to the scholarship kid, whose mom was the lunch lady. He got suspended quite a lot, almost lost out on his chance to stay at the school to play ball. It wasn't until he really became friends with Jax that things turned around for him."

Her heart broke for the picture Ryan painted of a young Pete. The man she knew was so kind and gentle she couldn't picture him getting into fights regularly. "What happened with his dad?" She was almost afraid of the answer.

Ryan smiled. "Pete's mom helped him to see the error of his ways."

"I knew I liked her," Kendall said. "Where are you going with all this? What does it have to do with Pete and I?"

Ryan rubbed the back of his neck uncomfortably. "Pete should really be the one talking to you about all this shit, not me, but I know he won't so—" He broke off. "You going to put the water on at least?"

"Oh my god seriously, just spill it already. You're building this up into something major and my brain is firing in a million directions with all these worst-case scenarios."

"No, it's nothing like that. It's just the way Pete grew up. He's got some issues about how smart he is and where he fits. Baseball makes sense to him. Everything else, not so much." Ryan stood up and grabbed a pot and started filling it at the pasta spigot. "Bottom line, I don't think he feels like he is good enough to keep you."

"So, he's just going to give up before we even really start? That's stupid."

"Agreed, but it's doesn't matter what we think, it matters what he thinks. Despite being a ballplayer, Pete hates anything that puts him on display because he always worries someone else could be better. With ball he knows he's the best. So that's easy."

"Why wouldn't he just tell me all this?" Kendall asked.

Ryan rolled his eyes. "Come on, Ken, what guy in his right mind would point out his flaws to the woman he's trying to impress?"

"I don't know. Being vulnerable can be sexy."

"Gross, please don't talk about what you think is sexy. I really don't need any of those images in my brain."

"Whatever." She chewed her bottom lip as she processed all that Ryan had shared. "So, you really think this all came down to Pete being scared of getting hurt and not because he didn't really want me?"

"I think the problem is he wants you too much. Not that I have any idea why." Ryan pinned her with a stare. The knowing big brother smirk on his face let her know he saw more than she'd wanted to share with him. "Maybe just give him a chance to prove to you he wants this to work. It's a big step for him. Maybe meet him halfway."

"It's a big step for me too," Kendall whispered.

"I know, kiddo, but you've never been one to run from anything. You always come up swinging, maybe show him what it looks like to fight for what you want."

"Maybe," she mumbled.

"That's all I ask." Ryan dropped a kiss on the top of her head. "I'm going to grab a quick shower before we eat."

"But the pasta will be ready soon."

"Oh, I thought maybe you'd bake it since you know that's my favorite." Ryan batted his eyes at her like a pathetic puppy and she laughed.

"Fine, go get your shower."

"You're the best. No one wonder Pete's crazy about you, sis," Ryan called as he walked down the hall.

But was he crazy enough about her?

CHAPTER EIGHTEEN

Monday morning, Kendall sat at her desk and stared at her emails. When she'd come to San Diego, she'd agreed to stay for a couple of weeks to see if she felt this job would be a good fit. The more time she spent with the creative team, the more she felt like she could make a real difference here. With her in charge, she truly felt this office could become the go-to boutique marketing company on the west coast. This opportunity was her chance to really prove herself.

But could she live in the same city as Pete? It was hard enough to keep him from her thoughts when she was in Atlanta and he was here, but in the same city? She sighed.

No, she wouldn't make this decision based on Pete. She needed to make it based on what was best for her and her career. But that was a lot easier to do when the team was on the road and a lot harder to do when they were home.

Her conversation with Ryan kept replaying over in her mind. Maybe she owed it to Pete to at least hear him out. But why did she always have to be the one to make compromises in a relationship? Just once, she wanted to be pursued.

"Kendall, there's a Max Gruber on line one for you," Simone's voice came over the intercom.

"Thanks, Simone, put him through."

Max Gruber, Max Gruber, why did she know that name? "Hi Mr. Gruber, this is Kendall Graves."

"Kendall hi, please call me Max. I am the CEO of Syn Underwear Corporation."

Holy shit. Syn Underwear was the most popular men's underwear brand on the market today. "Of course. What can I do for you, Max?"

"I have heard great things about you and was hoping we could sit down and talk about our marketing campaign."

She knew she was talented, but Max Gruber calling her out of the blue? That was some twilight zone shit right there. "Absolutely. I'd love to schedule a meeting with you. May I ask who referred you to me?"

"Of course. We're in negotiations with an athlete about doing some special endorsement ads and they spoke very highly of you."

Why wouldn't Ryan have mentioned he was in negotiations for an endorsement deal like Syn? "Are you looking for us to partner with you for this campaign?" Kendall held her breath. Signing a contract with Syn, even for one ad campaign, would put their boutique on the map. It would speed up her timelines exponentially.

What she had pictured as their five-year plan could be fast-tracked to two.

"Possibly, yes. I'm going to be brutally honest with you, Kendall. I want this athlete and they'll only agree to do the ad with you at the helm. We'd like to partner with you for this series of ads, and if you are as good as I've been told, then I hope this will lead to repeat business."

"Are you looking at print or TV?" Kendall reached into her drawer and pulled out a notepad and started scratching down ideas.

"Both. Would you have time for us to all have a meeting this week over Zoom?"

"Of course. Let me know your schedule and we can arrange something. There's no conflict with your office with me working on my brother's advertising campaign?"

"Your brother? Pete never mentioned that you were his sister."

Kendall placed her hand on her stomach. "Pete?" Why would Pete have recommended her? Pete hated the idea of doing endorsements like this. "Pete Saunders?"

"Yes. It's my understanding he has some reservations about doing this kind of media and felt you would be perfectly suited to create something that would fit both of our needs."

Kendall's mind spun. What was happening? Why would Pete be willing to do this? Why would he recommend her after everything?

"Are you still there, Kendall?" Max asked.

"Yes, of course. Sorry, just thinking about the possibilities."

Max's low chuckle slid over the line. "I have a good feeling about this. I think Pete may be right about you."

"You don't see a conflict with me working on the ad of a friend?"

"Not at all. I think in situations like these friends can pull things out of us we never imagined. From what Pete said and then speaking with you today, I'm looking forward to exploring this partnership for all of us. I'll have my secretary be in touch."

Kendall hung up the phone and sat back in her chair. What just happened?

She grabbed her phone and hit Pete's number on speed dial. The phone rang and went to voicemail. "Pete, hey, it's Kendall. I just got a call from Syn Under-wear. Can you call me, please?"

Twenty minutes later, her phone buzzed with a text message.

Pete: Sorry at practice. Any chance we could meet for dinner or something tonight to chat?

Kendall: You recommended me for an ad campaign?

Pete: Can we please just meet and talk?

Kendall: Fine

Pete: Restaurant or my place?

Kendal: Restaurant

Pete: 7? DeMarco's?

Kendall: Sounds good

Kendall leaned back in her chair and stared down at her phone as she tried to make sense of what was happening. Her heart skipped a beat at the thought of seeing Pete tonight. What was he going to say? Was she strong enough to listen? Was he doing this endorsement to make things up to her or as a peace offering?

She threw her head back. God, she had more questions than answers.

A light knock on her office door drew her out of her introspection. "Brad, hey, what can I do for you?"

"You had said you wanted to meet with the team regarding the diabetes medicine campaign at 2:00pm."

Kendall glanced up at the clock and winced when she saw it was already 2:15. "Shoot, sorry. I'll be right there."

She closed down her email and locked her computer, then grabbed her notepad and headed to the boardroom. At least she had something else to focus her attention on so she could temporarily forget about Pete.

Pete sat at a secluded table in DeMarco's. He silently nursed his beer as he waited for Kendall to arrive. When he'd left the house, he'd been worried about being late and making her wait. Unfortunately, he'd ended up showing up fifteen minutes early. Which meant fifteen painful minutes of worrying about what to say and how she would react.

He was swinging for the fences with this one, which meant he'd either knock it out of the park or he'd fall on his ass and fail. He rubbed his palms on his jeans as nerves coursed through him. The last thing he wanted to do was fail.

The server walked toward him with Kendall in tow, and Pete's mouth went dry. She looked incredible. Her caramel hair was curled softly, falling in waves down over her shoulders. Her green dress clung to her curves like it was made for her, and he smiled. Hopefully, the fact that she was wearing green was a good sign.

He stood when Kendall made it to the table.

"Kendall, thanks for coming. You look beautiful."

She smiled and a flush spread across her cheeks. "Thank you."

He was definitely going to take the blush as a good sign. Her dress pulled tight across her breasts as she shifted in her seat and he bit back a groan. The green color immediately made him think of the night she'd wrapped herself up in a green blanket after they'd had Facetime sex and he'd told her green was his new favorite color.

"How have you been? How's the job going?" Pete asked. He really hoped the job was everything she had hoped. He was banking on the fact that even if tonight didn't go well, Kendall would move to the city for the job and he would still have a chance to win her back.

"It's going really well. Now that Mark isn't there, I can see the unique personalities of all the staff. For all Mark's faults, he hired an amazing team."

"That's good. Do you think you're going to take the job?"

"It's looking that way, yes." Kendall shifted her body and her foot brushed against his shin as she crossed her legs beneath the table.

"So, Pete, I'm confused by the Syn endorsement."

The server stopped at the table. "Can I bring you something to drink?"

"I'll have a glass of your house white," Kendall replied.

Pete flicked his hand towards his beer. "I'm still good, thanks."

As soon as they were alone, Kendall pinned him with a stare. Her brown eyes pierced into him, and he was afraid she saw far more than he wanted her to.

"Syn? I thought you hated those kinds of ads?"

"Right." He exhaled a shaky breath. Go big or go home. "I do. But I don't hate you. In fact, how I feel about you is the exact opposite of hate."

"Okay, what does that have to do with you doing an underwear ad?"

Now that he was sitting across from Kendall and having to admit this out loud, it suddenly didn't seem like such a good idea.

"Spit it out, Pete. Why are you now willing to do this kind of ad? And why make working with me a condition?"

"I fucked up with you, Kendall. And I'm so goddamned sorry." He clenched his fingers to stop himself from reaching for her. "All I could think about was getting you back, and what could I do to get you to give me another chance? Then I was talking to Ryan and something he said made me realize I hadn't been fair to you. If I want a relationship with you, I have to put your needs first."

"Okay, and how does this ad put me first? Because of my career? My career will be fine without you giving me a pity contract."

"God, Kendall, no, this is the furthest thing from a pity contract. If anything, you'd be taking the job because you feel sorry for me." Pete shifted uncomfortably in his chair and looked back at her. She raised her eyebrows, waiting expectantly for him to continue.

"When you mentioned how you could market the shit out of a campaign with me half-naked, I thought you were crazy. The idea of a billboard sized picture of me in my underwear is mortifying. But not as mortifying as the idea of never holding you again, never seeing that smile directed at me or that secret laugh you do when you are thinking dirty thoughts." He reached across the table and grabbed her hand. When she didn't pull away, he pressed on. "The idea of a life without you by my side is unbearable. I don't know when it happened, Ken, but I am totally head over fucking heels in love with you and if it takes laying myself bare on a national scale to prove to you I'm willing to put you first, that nothing matters more to me than seeing you happy, I will gladly do it. Like Ryan said I have to be willing to humiliate myself to show you how I feel, and I am. I trust you, Kendall. You're the only person I could ever trust with an ad campaign like that and even though doing it scares the shit out of me, I trust you will make it okay. I trust that you'd have my back."

Kendall's eyes swam with tears as she looked at him, not saying a word. Pete held his breath as he waited for her to speak. When a tear broke free from her eye and dripped down her cheek, he reached up and brushed it off with his thumb.

Kendall grabbed his hand and held it against her cheek. She closed her eyes and let the tears flow down her face. He didn't know if this was a good thing or bad. Afraid to ruin anything, he sat silently.

"You don't have to do the ad to prove this to me, Pete."

"But it would be good for your career, right?"

"It would be amazing for my career, but that doesn't mean you have to do something that makes you so uncomfortable."

"I trust you, Ken. If you're with me, I know it will be fine. Like I said, I want to prove to you how important you are and how much I am willing to put you first."

He stood up and pulled his chair around the table and placed it beside hers. Grabbing the arm of her chair, he spun the seat so she was facing him. He took both of her hands in his and leaned forward, silently begging her to hear what he was having trouble saying.

"There is nothing more important to me than you, Kendall. I'm sorry I got scared and bolted, but I want to make it up to you and prove to you what you mean to me."

"You don't have to prove anything to me."

"No, I do. You were right. You deserve someone who will fight for you, who'll make an ass of themselves for you. This is me stepping up and going all in. I just hope I'm not too late."

She stared at him, her eyes filled with pain and longing but also hope. It was that glimmer of hope he held onto.

"Trust me, Ken, I'm in this."

Kendall wiped the tears from her face as a slow smile spread across her lips. "I do trust you, Pete. And you're not too late." She sniffed and tilted her head to the side as she smiled at him like she was truly seeing him and liked what she saw. His heart pounded in his chest.

"I'm sorry too, Pete. I got my feelings hurt and shut things down and didn't give you a chance to explain, and as Ryan pointed out to me, I'm not the only one with baggage." She shifted forward in her seat so their knees touched. "I love you so much and I'm all in, too."

Pete spread his legs wider, so Kendall's knees slipped between his as he pulled her chair closer. Reaching up, he threaded his fingers through her hair and drew her face toward him. "I love you, Kendall," he whispered against her lips a moment before he pressed his against hers.

Breaking their kiss, he rested his forehead against hers and closed his eyes, breathing her breath. He'd come so close to losing her, now that he had her back, he was never letting her go. "You're coming home with me," he told her.

"There's no place I'd rather be."

EPILOGUE

Kendall giggled as she heard Pete cussing from behind the changing screen. She walked over to the makeshift changing area. "Everything okay in there?" she asked.

"Can you come in here for a second?"

She snickered at the pained tone of his voice. Peeking her head around the screen, she saw Pete in the Syn underwear for the first time. "Day-um." Her eyes hungrily raked over his body. Pete in his normal underwear was a sight to behold, Pete in these bad boys. Priceless. This campaign would sell itself.

Pete pulled the crotch of his underwear away from himself. "Can you not look at me like that please," he growled.

"What? You look amazing."

"I look indecent. When they said a pocket for my balls, I didn't think they meant it would shove it all front and center. This looks ridiculous."

"Trust me, babe, it definitely doesn't look ridiculous." She walked over to him and placed her hands on his chest. "Relax. You look hot. You said you trusted me on this ad campaign, so trust me. I promise you look amazing." She reached down and grabbed his hand. "Now come on so you can get some shine on your chest."

"I need makeup on my chest now? Jesus," he muttered.

She giggled and tugged him out from behind the screen. "Don't be a baby."

As they walked towards the makeup artist, the photographer whistled. "Guess we don't need to stuff him with a sock."

"I'm out," Pete said and spun on his heel.

Kendall gripped his arm and held him in place. "Stop. Just ignore him, focus on me and we'll be done in no time."

He turned around and stepped closer as he looked down at her. "Fine, but you owe me for this."

She pressed her body against his and whispered. "Believe me, I'll make it worth your while."

Pete groaned and put some space between their bodies. "Not cool, Ken, when I'm standing here with my junk on full display."

Seeing how uncomfortable this all made him and how willing he was to do this for her made her love him all the more. "Then quit messing around and go get your photos done so we can get home and I can give you your reward."

He shook his head and stepped away. She swatted his ass as he walked past. "Show me some smolder, Zip," she taunted.

Pete flipped up his middle finger over his shoulder.

"Pete Saunders, did you just finger me?"

He turned, quirked his eyebrow and flashed her a sexy smirk. "Not yet, I didn't."

And that was all it took. She pressed her legs together as moisture instantly pooled in her core. God, this man. She licked her lips, then remembering where she was, she pointed her finger. "Behave and get to work."

"Yes, boss," he teased.

Kendall shook her head. "Love you," she called out.

"Love you too, Ken." Pete walked towards the photographer. "All right, let's get this over with."

THE END

For upcoming releases, exclusive content, contests and giveaways, be sure to <u>subscribe to my newsletter</u> http://www.laurenfraser.com/newsletter.

Plus as a newsletter subscriber you'll get access to a newsletter subscriber-only FREE book.

Want to read how Kendall's big brother, pitcher Ryan Graves falls? Keep swiping for a preview of <u>Throwing the Curve by Lauren Fraser. Book 3 in the Playing for Keeps Series.</u>

EXCERPT
THROWING
THE CURVE

W as it too soon to be meeting his teammates? Peyton glanced over at Simon. Did she even want to meet his friends? What if they didn't like her? What if she didn't like them? God, she wasn't even sure how she was feeling about Simon, let alone his friends. Gah.

He winked and reached across the center console to place his hand on her knee. "Relax babe, they're going to love you."

"Remind me whose party this is again?" she asked as she slid her hand nervously down her lap, smoothing out her skirt. She clasped Simon's hand, hoping it would calm her nerves. Going to a party with him felt like a big step. One she wasn't sure they were ready for.

"It's a housewarming for Sanchez. He's new this season and plays left field. He just bought this place. It should be pretty low key, just a few of the guys from the team and their dates."

"Does he have a first name?"

Simon chuckled. "Yeah, Tony."

The car pulled up in front of a sprawling rancher in Mission Bay. Peyton scanned the front of the house, her eyes lingering on the beautiful old rose bushes beneath the front windows. Just like the ones at her grandma's house. She could almost smell them from here and it instantly transported her back to making rose water on summer break as a kid.

She pushed open the car door and rounded the front of the vehicle.

Simon stopped beside her and made a rough noise in his throat, and she turned toward him. "What?"

"Nothing. I thought he would have bought something a little newer. This thing looks like it was built in the eighties."

Peyton rolled her eyes. "It doesn't look that old." Peyton once again scanned the front of the house. "It's lovely and the location is fantastic. There's a great public beach right down the street." She'd love to live in a place like this. Who wouldn't?

"Yeah, a public beach," Simon scoffed.

"Oh my god, could you be a bigger snob? Seriously, there's nothing wrong with a public beach. That's where most of us common folk go to swim."

He wrapped his arm around her waist and pulled her closer to him. "Yeah, but you're not common anymore, baby. You're with me now. I don't do common."

She tensed at his tone. They'd only been dating for a few weeks, and she'd never dated someone with money before. She wasn't sure if the slight jabs at her economic level were normal, or his way of trying to brag, or what it was, but it grated. "Let's go inside."

He placed his hand on the small of her back as they made their way down the side of the house. Laughing and splashing sounds drifted toward her as they rounded the corner and into the large backyard. Peyton stopped as she looked around to get her bearings. Holy cow. Older home or not, this backyard alone was worth buying the house. A large in-ground pool with several people splashing around took up the right side of the yard. A sweeping decorative cement patio curved around the pool. Off to the left was a beautiful, covered area with a fireplace and a large flatscreen tv hanging above it. Who had a TV outside? This was whole other level stuff than what she was used to.

"Andy," a deep voice yelled, drawing her attention toward the barbecue.

Simon walked toward the man working the grill. "Hey Tony, thanks for having us."

"Glad you could make it." Tony glanced over at her. His dark brown eyes scanned her from head to toe in a thorough male assessment. He smiled and stuck out his hand. "Hi, I'm Tony, you must be Carmella?"

Ouch. Peyton's shoulders tensed. Who the hell was Carmella?

Simon laughed. "Nah, man, this is Peyton."

"Oh sorry, my mistake. I'm new, so still trying to figure out who everyone is."

She glanced over at Simon, and he rolled his eyes like Tony was an idiot for getting her name wrong. He smacked Tony on the back. "No problem, man, it happens. We're going to grab a drink," Simon said.

"Sure, help yourself. There's beer and wine in the fridge there," he said, pointing to the small stainless fridge in the outdoor kitchen. "And I think Saunders is in the kitchen watching Kendall make margaritas if you want one of those."

"What'll it be?" Simon asked.

"A margarita sounds great, actually," she replied.

They wove their way inside to the kitchen. "Hey hey, looks like this is where the party is," Simon called out.

Five heads swiveled toward them. "Hey Andy."

Peyton scanned the group. Good lord, she had not been prepared for the testosterone flowing off these men as she they all swung their attention toward her.

"Can we grab a couple of those, Kendall?" Simon asked.

"Told ya if you stood around talking instead of blending you'd be stuck making these all night." A brown-haired guy she was pretty sure was the shortstop Pete Saunders, smacked the woman making drinks on the butt.

Peyton glanced over at Simon. Was he going to introduce her?

Instead, he stepped up to the island and grabbed a tortilla chip from the bowl and dipped it into the salsa. Okay, apparently manners weren't his strong suit. She stared at him.

Wow, he was like a different person when he was alone with her than he was in front of his teammates. The Simon she knew had pursued her hard. He'd been sweet and attentive. This 'Andy' as his teammates called him, was a bit of an arrogant jerk. She eyed him speculatively and wondered which one was the real man.

She stepped up to the counter. "Hi, sorry. Looks like Simon isn't going to introduce us, so I'm Peyton."

Simon glanced over at her. "Sorry, babe." He placed his hand on her hip. "Peyton, this is Gonzo, Smitty, Zip, Kendall and" He paused and turned to the man standing on the other side of Peyton. Wow, he was gorgeous and looked seriously pissed. She sucked in a breath as ice-blue eyes drilled into her.

Simon snorted beside her. "The guy glaring at us is Undertaker."

"I told you not to fucking call me that," glaring guy growled.

Apparently, there was no love lost between these two.

"Why not? It's perfect." Simon glanced around at the other men around the island. "Don't you guys think it fits him perfectly?"

"Ah, not really, no," Pete answered.

Gonzo wrinkled his nose and shook his head. "I think Ryan is good. No need for a nickname, really."

"Ace works," Smitty piped in.

"Come on, you guys, just because Ryan has no sense of humor doesn't mean the name isn't perfect," Simon said as he picked up another tortilla and dipped it.

She turned to Simon. "Sorry, why would Undertaker be perfect?"

"Come on, babe, I thought you were a ball fan."

She bristled at the mocking tone of his voice. She definitely was not a fan of Simon with the boys. "I am. I just have to agree with them that Undertaker sounds more like he's a wrestler than a pitcher."

"How'd you know I was the pitcher?" grumpy guy asked.

She glanced over at him and again was struck by his piercing blue eyes. Sheesh, she'd seen all these guys on TV when she watched the games and the interviews, but she hadn't been prepared for them up close. The TV did not do Ryan Graves justice. "Like Simon said, I watch sports. It's kind of a job requirement to understand the game."

Ryan's eyes ran down her body, and she fought the urge to cross her arms over her chest. He wasn't looking at her like she was a desirable woman, but like something he found on the bottom of his shoe. What the hell was that about?

"Yeah, what kind of job is that?" he mocked.

"Oh fuck," Smitty mumbled.

Ryan's stare whipped off her and over to Smitty. "What?"

"Incoming," Smitty muttered and nodded toward the doors behind them.

"Fuck," Simon groaned and took several steps away from her just as the sliding glass door opened and three women walked in.

"Surprise," the curvy brunette called as she sashayed toward Simon and leaned in for a kiss when she reached him

Peyton felt like she'd been kicked in the stomach. He had a girlfriend? What the heck? She looked over at Simon and the beautiful woman now wrapped around his side. He refused to make eye contact with. Mother F'er. She shook her head as a sick feeling swept through her stomach.

"Hi everybody," the woman called.

"Hey Carmella," Ryan said from beside her.

Carmella eyed Peyton up and down. "Who are you?" Carmella asked.

"That's Peyton. She's Undertaker's date," Simon said.

"No," Ryan growled.

"Right, right, sorry we agreed I wouldn't call you that." Simon laughed. He looked down at Carmella and made a face. "He has no sense of humor."

Carmella squealed. "Oh, my gosh, I've never met one of Ryan's girls before. This is so exciting. I'm Simon's wife, Carmella."

"His wife?" she asked. Her ears buzzed, the noise getting louder and louder. She looked around the room trying to get her bearings. Her mind raced to catch up with what was happening in front of her. Was she being punked? This was like some bad movie.

Carmella smiled and waved her hand in the air. A huge diamond sparkled on her ring finger. "Seven years."

Oh my god, she was a home wrecker. How had this happened? He was married? Her eyes flashed to his bare ring finger. Why didn't he wear a ring like a normal person?

"Who's watching the kids?" Simon asked his wife.

"You have kids?" Peyton squeaked.

"Yep, three of them," Carmella replied to Peyton before turning to her husband and patting his chest. "Don't worry, when Chelan called and asked me to come, she'd already okayed it with her nanny, so they are all at our place."

Peyton placed a hand on her stomach. Oh, my god she was going to be sick. She needed to get out of here. Her eyes flashed around the room. "Where's the bathroom?" she asked.

The woman across the island from her, Kendall possibly, pointed to the staircase on the right. "It's upstairs at the end of the hall. You can't miss it."

"Thanks," she murmured before making a beeline out of the room.

Once inside the washroom, she leaned her hands against the counter and dropped her head. How had this happened? How could she be dating a married man? She'd asked him about his relationship status, and he'd told her he was single. She cringed. No, he'd said there was no one she'd needed to worry about, and she'd stupidly thought that meant he was single. Paired with the naked ring finger and she'd figured it was fine. Sure, she'd expected he might be a bit of a player because he was a professional athlete, but she'd thought that meant more he wouldn't get serious about her, which is why they still hadn't officially slept together despite several weeks of dating.

She covered her mouth and groaned. Ew, she'd had oral sex with a married man. Gross.

She sat down on the edge of the tub. Oh my god, she was the other woman. Nausea rolled in her gut. No, no, no, no, no. This was not happening. She couldn't be the other woman.

An affair had ripped her parents apart. There was no way she was going to be that person. She'd done everything right. How could this happen?

She looked around the washroom. Great and now she was stuck in a stranger's bathroom with the guy she was having an affair with downstairs with his wife. She was a home wrecker. Oh my god, it was official. She was no better than the women her dad had been with.

She had to get out of here. But how?

With trembling hands, she pulled her phone out of her purse. Her vision blurred as she tried to pull up her contacts. Great, and now she was crying. She wiped her face, took a shuddering breath, and dialed her best friend Rayne. The second Rayne picked up, she whispered, "He's married."

"Who's married?" Rayne whispered back.

"Simon," Peyton whispered louder.

"Holy shit, he's married," Rayne yelled. "Sorry. He's married?" she whispered.

"Why are you whispering?"

"I don't know. You were whispering so I went with it," Rayne answered.

"Well, I'm hiding in the bathroom at a party. That's why I'm whispering," Peyton replied. She looked over at the small bathroom window. Shoot, there was no way she could squeeze out of that little thing.

Oh god, she couldn't breathe. Why was it so hot in here? She grabbed the edge of her shirt and fanned herself.

"Pey, you still there?" Rayne's voice cut through the buzzing in her ears.

"Yeah, just trying to figure out how I'm going to get out of here. Can you come pick me up?"

"Sorry sweetie, I'm at work and have a client coming in ten minutes."

"Awesome," she grumbled. Getting an uber all the way out here and back to her place would cost a month's rent.

"How the hell can he be married? Didn't you ask?"

"Of course I asked. I'm not an idiot," she snapped. "Sorry, you didn't deserve that. I'm just...god. I don't know what I am. Pissed off, embarrassed." She rubbed her hands across her face. Gross, why was she so sweaty? She glanced at her flushed face in the mirror. This day was just getting better and better. Now she was having like a hot flash or something. She flapped her arms to try to cool herself down. "Rayne, I've got to get out of here," she whispered as the panic roared in her chest again.

"Just breathe, it'll be fine."

"It's not going to be fine. The jerk told his wife I was Ryan Graves' date."

"Is he cute?"

"Are you freakin' kidding me right now? "

"What? I'm just asking. I mean, clearly you can't date Simon now, and it's been a hot minute since you got laid. So..."

"Not helpful, Rayne. Like at all."

"Okay, so maybe your new date could give you a ride or something?"

"Yeah, sure, the guy who glared at me like he hated me on sight is going to give me a ride."

"Seriously, he glared at you?" Rayne asked.

"Yep, but totally makes sense now since he thought I was the other woman." She groaned. "Which I totally am." Tears welled up in her eyes and she looked up at the ceiling. "God, Rayne, help me. What am I supposed to do? I can't keep hiding in the bathroom forever. People will start to think it's weird."

No sooner had the words left her mouth than there was a knock on the door, followed by a deep male voice. "You okay in there?"

"Crap, Rayne," she whispered. "Umm yep, fine, be out in a second," she called to the stranger at the door. Could this day get any worse? "I gotta go," she whispered to Rayne.

"Call me when you get home," Rayne said.

Peyton hung up the phone and glanced at herself in the mirror. Perfect, she looked like a hot mess. She splashed some cold water on her face and looked at herself again. Awesome that made it worse. Now her face was all blotchy. Oh god, kill me now.

Taking a deep breath, she grabbed the doorknob and pulled the door open. Of course, it had to be him. Icy-glare Graves.

"It's all yours," she said as she tried to step by him.

"You okay?" he asked.

"Not really." Laughter drifted up from downstairs. There was no way she was going back down there. "Do you know the address so I can get an uber?"

He smirked at her. "Didn't sign on for meeting the wife today, hey?"

"Didn't know there was a wife."

"Yeah right," he scoffed.

Peyton's shoulders tensed. Who the heck did this guy think he was judging her like this? "Obviously I didn't, or I wouldn't be here."

"Come on now, that's not entirely true. There are at least two women in the pool out back that are dating guys they know are married, because they are fake dating other guys on the team. I just have no intention of being one of those guys."

"Are you kidding me?"

"Nope." He looked her up and down and shook his head. "So what, you didn't google Andy before you started dating?"

"No, why would I?"

"Right, you expect me to believe you started dating a famous athlete and didn't look him up online? Please."

"I didn't," she snapped. Although now she really wished she had. "I didn't think I had to."

"Sure." He laughed. "Sell that one to someone else, sweetheart."

"Are you calling me a liar?" She glared at the man in front of her. What an arrogant prick. How dare he stand there judging her when his friends were the kind of guys who behaved like this?

"Just calling it like I see it, sweetheart."

"Screw you," she seethed.

"Not really interested. Thanks."

Peyton's jaw clenched. This guy was unbelievable. "I'm going to need you to move out of my way."

"What, so you can join the party? I'm not having you go down there and embarrass Carmella in front of everyone."

"Embarrass Carmella? Right." She took a deep breath. "You have no reason to believe me, but I have no intention of hurting Carmella. Simon might be a jerk, but his wife did nothing to me. I need to get out of here. Can you help me do that? Please?"

He stared at her for several minutes before finally nodding his head. "Sure come on." At the top of the stairs, he paused and glanced back at her. "What was your name again?"

"Peyton."

"Peyton. Got it." He looked down the stairs and sighed. "Alright Peyton, let's do this."

Why did he have to make it feel like they were facing a firing squad instead of his teammates? This didn't bode well for her getting out of here unscathed.

The moment they stepped into the kitchen, the women descended on her like a pack of hyenas. "So, Simon said you run the sports program for kids that he volunteers at. Is that how you met Ryan?" Carmella asked.

"Uh... how... uh... Ryan and I met?" she stammered.

"Yes, how did you two meet?" Carmella prodded.

"Umm..." She looked around the room at all the people staring at her expectantly, waiting for her response. She didn't want to lie. God, she didn't want to be here at all.

A hand brushed across her shoulder and she glanced back at Ryan. "Peyton isn't feeling very good, so I'm going to run her home and come back. So maybe we can save the inquisition for another time, hey, Carm?" He smiled at Simon's wife.

Carmella wrinkled her nose at him. "It wasn't an inquisition. I'm just curious about how you met." Carmella's eyes warmed as she smiled at Ryan. "You never bring women to these things, so of course when you do we know she must be special. I want to make sure she deserves you."

"Thanks, Carm, I appreciate it. You don't have to worry about me."

"Of course I do. You're the sweetest guy I know." Carmella turned to Peyton. "You better be good to him."

"Jesus, Carm, he's a grown as man, not a puppy dog. Maybe he brought her because she's hot and he wants to fuck her," Simon said.

Peyton sucked in a breath. Did he really just say that?

Carmella elbowed Simon in the gut and he let out an oomph sound.

"You're such a dick," Ryan growled. His entire body was tense against Peyton's side, like it was taking everything in him to stay in place. This stranger was more protective of her than the man she was supposed to be dating.

"What?" Simon asked.

Yeah, if they hadn't been done before she found out about his wife, seeing what a douche he was around his friends would have solidified the deal for her. Peyton stared at the man in front of her. What had she been thinking dating him?

"Carm, I will never understand what you see in this guy. But it's always a pleasure to see you," Ryan said then turned back to Peyton. "You ready to go?"

"Yeah, definitely," she replied.

Ryan pressed his hand against her back and guided her toward the door. Who knew her knight in shining armor would be the one person at the party who hated her?

Buy Link

About Author

Lauren Fraser resides in British Columbia, Canada, with her husband, two children, and two dogs. When she's not busy writing, Lauren loves to spend time with her family outside—camping, hiking and paddle boarding.

Lauren writes about love and relationships in many different forms, but in the end, she's a sucker for a happy ending. She is multi-published and loves to hear from her readers. For the latest updates, visit her website.

Website http://www.laurenfraser.com/